# RESISTING *my* ROOMMATE



T.K. LEIGH WRITING AS
## TRACY LEIGH

# RESISTING MY ROOMMATE



Published by Carpe Per Diem Publishing, Inc

For a full list of all of Tracy's books, including recommended reading order, please visit her website:

www.tracyleighbooks.com

Books and reading order for her spicy billionaire romance alter ego, T.K. Leigh, can be found here:

www.tkleighauthor.com

For exclusive sales and excerpts,
sign up for Tracy Leigh's VIP list!

https://www.tracyleighbooks.com/subscribe

Or scan the code below

*To everyone looking for a place to belong...*

Some of the author's books may contain content that could be triggering for sensitive readers. For a full list of content warnings for each book and/or series, please visit her website.

https://geni.us/TKLContentWarnings

# ONE

## *Jude*

"**W**ant another?" the bartender asks as I sit at the counter of a darkened bar.

Just like I do on this day every year.

I wish it could be like any other day.

I *want* it to be like any other day.

It's not. I doubt it ever will be.

I give the bartender a curt nod, and he takes my empty rocks glass, replacing it with a fresh one. Raising the amber liquid to my lips, I allow the familiar burn to course through me, trying to drown the grief that still plagues me.

Especially today.

The sound of excited voices interrupts the memories playing in my mind like a bad movie, and I glance behind me as a group of women file inside, all of them dressed for a night out on the town. The sashes and tacky necklaces they wear make it clear it's a bachelorette party.

*Great.*

Facing forward, I do my best to tune them out as they order shots and toast the bride-to-be's future happiness. I can't help but scoff at the naïve notion that happiness is all you need for a marriage to work. They have no idea how fleeting happiness is.

As I tip back my glass so I can down my drink and make a hasty exit, I sense someone approach. Glancing to my right, I rake my gaze down the tall blonde wearing a fitted white dress, a makeshift veil askew on her head, along with a sash that reads "Bride-to-Be". Based on the giant stone sparkling on her left hand, her future husband must do well for himself.

"Nice rock," I say.

She darts her head toward me. "What's that?"

I nod at her hand. "Your ring. It's nice."

"Thanks," she answers with what seems like forced enthusiasm. Which intrigues me.

"When's the big day?" I ask after the bartender takes her order for an ice water with lemon. Another surprise, since the rest of her friends seem to be on a mission to get as drunk as possible. Not her, though. In fact, she doesn't seem to be celebrating at all.

"Saturday." She smiles, but it doesn't reach her eyes.

As the owner of a brewery and taproom a short distance from here, I've dealt with my fair share of bachelorette parties. Usually, the bride is gushing over the idea of walking down the aisle and saying "I do".

Not this woman.

"You don't seem too excited," I blurt out before I can stop myself.

"What makes you say that?" she challenges, facing me.

I shrug, taking another sip of my whiskey. "Most brides are practically glowing, babbling about floral arrangements or how their fiancé is the most perfect man on the planet."

I study her for a beat, noticing how she fidgets with her engagement ring. Like it's more of a burden than a symbol of a man's undying love.

Or maybe I just want to see it that way.

"You seem more… reserved."

"Maybe I don't feel like babbling," she replies, her tone dry. "I'm excited about getting married."

A humorless laugh escapes my throat. "Why's that?"

"I found someone who makes me happy. Why wouldn't I want to marry him?"

"Society loves to tell us it's what we're supposed to do. Doesn't it?" I lift my glass back to my lips. "Find someone, settle down, play house. Doesn't mean it's the right path."

"Sounds like someone's a little jaded."

"Maybe. Or maybe I'm a realist. There's this ridiculous societal pressure that, in order to live a complete life, you need to be married. If you ask me, it's all bullshit."

She grabs the glass the bartender leaves on the counter and brings the straw up to her full, red lips. A part of me wonders how they'd look wrapped around my dick instead of that straw.

I blame the whiskey for even thinking it.

"I'm going out on a limb here and guessing your girlfriend or wife left you." Her voice pulls me back to the present, giving me a dose of reality.

She doesn't realize how right she is. But I have no intention of talking about the worst time of my life with a complete stranger, even if I technically brought her question upon myself. Instead, I do what I always do in these situations. I deflect.

"People get married because they think it'll solve something — loneliness, insecurity, fear of missing out, or that getting married will make them whole. It doesn't."

"Sorry to burst your bubble, but I'm not getting married for any of those reasons."

"No?"

She squares her shoulders defiantly. "No."

"Then why are you?"

"Because I love him."

"Love," I scoff. "That's an even worse reason to get married than loneliness or fear of missing out."

"Why do you think that?"

I lean back in my seat, letting out a dry laugh. "Where do I start?"

She arches an expectant brow and fixes her eyes on me, waiting for whatever pearls of wisdom I'm about to impart on her. I take a moment, running a hand through my hair as I consider all the reasons the mere idea of love makes my skin itch.

"For one, love is temporary. It's like a sparkler on the Fourth of July. Bright, dazzling, but gone in a flash. You may think it's going to last forever, but eventually, it burns out. And what are you left with? A stick and a lot of smoke. Nothing real. Nothing of substance."

She tilts her head, a small frown forming on her lips, but she doesn't interrupt. She wants to hear this, and thanks to all the whiskey I've had, I'm on a roll.

"Two," I continue, holding up two fingers for emphasis, "love's a damn liar. It makes you believe things are better than they are. It's like a pair of rose-colored glasses that hide all the cracks and warning signs. You convince yourself the other person is perfect and you're meant to be together. Sooner or later, the glasses come off. When they do, reality hits harder than a two-ton truck."

"But isn't that the beauty of love?" she asks softly, taking a sip of her water. "That despite any flaws, you still care for each other and want to be together?"

"It's not the flaws that get you in the end," I

argue, my words slurring slightly. "It's the expectations love builds up. You have these pre-conceived notions about what a relationship should be, how your life is supposed to look. When it doesn't meet those expectations — because it never will — you're left disappointed and bitter. That's when the fights start. And let me tell you, love turns real fucking ugly when it's backed into a corner."

She takes another sip of water, still watching me with interest. "Love is just a fantasy. Is that it?"

"Fantasy, illusion, call it what you want," I reply with a dismissive wave of my hand. "It's unreliable. Fleeting. And the worst part? People use it as an excuse to ignore all the practical reasons they shouldn't get married. Love makes people do stupid things, like tie their whole damn life to someone else when they barely know themselves."

"So we're just supposed to play it safe?" There's a spark of fire in her voice I find intriguing. "Never take risks?"

I lean in closer, my tone steady but firm. "I'm saying if you're going to gamble, at least know the odds. And love? You'd have better luck spending your night at the roulette table and letting it all ride on a single number."

Silence hangs between us for what feels like an eternity, her expression a mixture of frustration and something I can't quite put my finger on. Maybe I've pushed too far. Maybe I sound like an asshole.

Who am I kidding? I'm *positive* I sound like an ass.

But this is my truth. I've seen what happens when people let love dictate their decisions. I've been there.

In many ways, I still am.

"Maybe you're just scared," she offers softly. Sweetly. "Scared of hoping for something better. Something real."

Her words hit me like a sucker punch, catching me off guard. I'm not sure what I expected her to say, but it certainly wasn't this. Didn't expect this complete stranger to see through all the bullshit.

But I'll never admit that. Not to her or anyone else.

"Believe what you want."

I shift in my seat, feeling exposed under her intense stare. As if she's slowly peeling back each of my layers one by one, revealing parts of me I've kept hidden for years. It unnerves me.

Yet there's also a sense of comfort in being seen so deeply by someone again. But I quickly push the thought away, using the burn of the whiskey to distract myself from the strange sensation bubbling inside of me in response to this woman. This…stranger.

"I appreciate your concern." She finally looks away, and I feel like I can breathe again. "But I'm going to take my chances. Thanks for the chat and the interesting…perspective."

"That's what I'm here for. Perspective." I finish

the rest of my drink and stand, tossing several bills onto the counter to cover my tab. "Good luck with your upcoming wedding." I head toward the door, my steps wavering from the alcohol.

"And good luck with whatever it is you're trying to forget," she calls out over the sound of nineties music blaring.

I pause, glancing over my shoulder and locking my eyes with hers for several moments.

Then I face forward and continue into the night, letting it swallow me whole.

# TWO

## Abbey

The afternoon sunlight pours through the tall, arched windows of the bridal suite, casting soft, golden beams that dance across the floor. The room smells faintly of gardenias, a sweet scent that's supposed to be calming but does little to settle the knot twisting in my stomach.

The knot that's been there since running into the stranger at the bar the other night. His words still linger in the recesses of my mind, making me examine my reasons for getting married through a microscope.

Am I only marrying Carson to check off a box?

One minute, I tell myself it's more than that and to forget about the bitter ramblings of a man who's obviously been burned before.

The next, I can't help but wonder if there's some truth to his assertions.

I take a deep breath, shaking off the mere thought. It's just pre-wedding jitters. Everyone gets them, right?

I'm not marrying Carson out of some delusional fairytale fantasy. He's always been incredibly supportive of me. Hell, when I was laid off last year, he was my rock, urging me not to stress about finding a new job while also planning our wedding. Granted, he makes a really good living as a financial planner and can afford to support both of us, but the fact he routinely puts my wellbeing first shows how thoughtful he is.

Still, there's a weight on my chest that won't go away. What if the stranger was right? Am I only getting married because I think it will fix what's broken?

"Knock knock. Are you decent?"

I snap out of my thoughts and shift my attention to the closed door.

"Come in," I call out.

My closest friend, Maia, slips into the room, her yellow bridesmaid dress swishing with her steps as she approaches me.

"Are you ready for your big day?" she asks, her eyes shining with excitement as she adjusts a button on the back of my wedding gown.

The crystals adorned to the fabric shimmer in the

light as it cascades in layers of satin and tulle, hugging the curves of my body before flaring out in a dramatic train behind me.

"As ready as I'll ever be." I let out a shaky breath, smoothing a hand down my stomach.

"You have nothing to worry about. Carson's a good man."

Maia would know, having worked with him at the investment firm for the past five years. In fact, it's how we became close friends. When Carson and I started dating, we'd often go on double dates with Maia and her husband. Now Maia and I plan our own outings without the guys.

"He is. Isn't he?" I remark, my nerves causing my words to come out in a rush.

"One of the best." She holds my gaze with a reassuring smile. "Are you ready? The photographer is waiting to do the first look photos."

I draw in another deep breath, pushing away the anxiety that threatens to suffocate me, blaming it on the wedding dress instead.

Giving Maia a small nod, I reply, "Let's go."

With a gentle tug, she leads me down the hallway and into the spacious main room of the rustic building perched on the edge of Lake Tahoe. The walls are made of reclaimed wood, giving off a cozy cabin feel while still maintaining an air of sophistication — one of the main reasons I chose this spot for today. The breathtaking view of the crystal-clear lake and majestic snow-covered mountains in the distance only adds to the romance of this place.

"Abbey…," Jennifer, the photographer, greets us the second we emerge from the hallway. "You look beautiful."

"Thank you." I glance around the space to find the waitstaff busy setting all the tables in preparation for the upcoming reception.

"Let's take a few solo shots before we bring in Carson."

"Of course."

Maia stays by my side, helping to maneuver my dress while Jennifer snaps away, capturing every moment against the backdrop of the shimmering lake. I'm grateful for the distraction. I don't have to think. Just have to do what she tells me.

Once she places me on one side of a brick wall separating the lounge area from the main room, she looks at Maia. "Can you go fetch the groom now?"

Maia nods eagerly and scurries down the hallway, her footsteps echoing through the cavernous space. Jennifer continues snapping photos of me while I try to tune out everything else. The ever-present knot in my stomach. The anxiety making me lightheaded. The question about whether this is really what I want.

Of course it is.

Like Maia just reminded me. Carson is a good man.

"Where is she?" Jennifer remarks, pulling me back

to the present. "It shouldn't take her this long to find Carson. Should it?"

Now that the click of her shutter no longer echoes over the space, it's eerily silent.

Well, that's not entirely true.

In the distance, a steady thumping grows louder and louder with each passing second. My face heats, my heart dropping to the pit of my stomach.

"Excuse me," I say to Jennifer, gathering the skirt of my dress in my hands as I walk in the direction of the sound. The rhythmic thud echoes off the walls, making my steps falter slightly.

As I grow near, it gets louder and more frenzied, a mixture of heavy breathing, hushed giggles, and labored grunts. But amongst it all, one sound stands out — a low breathy moan that is all too familiar.

A moan I've heard many times before.

I inch closer to the groomsmen suite as a soft voice calls out Carson's name, leaving no question in my mind precisely who's on the other side.

And what they're doing.

I place my hand on the knob, expecting it to be locked. After all, it would be foolish of them to leave the door unlocked while sneaking around behind my back just minutes before our wedding.

But just like I was wrong about Carson's faithfulness, I'm wrong about this, too.

The knob gives way, and I push the door open, revealing a scene that leaves me speechless. Carson's tuxedo is disheveled as he thrusts into Maia like a man possessed.

For a moment, I don't feel anything, as if my mind has disconnected from my body. I'm not sure why I'm surprised by this turn of events. My mother didn't want me, abandoning me on my father's doorstep when I was just fifteen. He wasn't much better, since he already had a family of his own and didn't know what to do with me.

Most of my life, I've felt like I'm not good enough.

Like I don't belong.

I guess I don't belong here, either.

At the realization, something inside me snaps. It's like a dam breaking. All the nervousness, doubt, and fear comes rushing out in a torrent of uncontrollable laughter.

Carson and Maia whip their heads toward me, their eyes wide with a mixture of shock and embarrassment.

"Abbey. Shit." Carson's face instantly turns a sickly shade of white as he scrambles to cover himself before advancing toward me. "This isn't what it looks like—"

I hold up a hand to stop him from coming any closer. "Oh, it's exactly what it looks like." I shake my head. "What a fucking cliché."

Spinning from them, I hurry toward the bridal suite, locking myself inside so I can gather my things without interruption.

"Abbey, please!" Carson begs, the desperation and urgency in his voice echoing off the walls. "Let's talk about this. No need to jump to conclusions. There's a perfectly good explanation for what you thought you saw." He bangs on the door, frantically jiggling the locked knob.

"He's right. It's not what you think," Maia chimes in, her own voice laced with anxiety, most likely over the prospect of her husband finding out.

Or worse, their boss.

I hope he finds out and fires them both, considering Carson is technically her superior.

"I'm sure there *is* a good explanation." I sling my bag over my shoulder and open the door, pinning them with a glare. "I'm guessing it's the same reason you've been working late these past few months, too. It explains all the times the two of you disappeared during a party, claiming you needed to discuss something work-related. In a way, I guess it wasn't that far off." I smirk at the woman I thought to be a close friend and confidant. "Pretending he's any good in bed can be a lot of work."

My words leave both of them momentarily speechless, and I spin, hurrying down the hallway and into the main dining room. The waitstaff watch with curiosity as I pass them, but I don't care.

All I do care about is getting as far away from this place as possible.

With my keys clutched in my hand, I dash to my

SUV and climb behind the wheel, stuffing the layers of my skirt in around me.

"Where are you going?" Carson calls after me.

"Away from here," I shout back. "And you."

"Think about the guests," he begs in a last-ditch effort as I'm about to shut the door. "There are important people here. Higher ups at my firm who are expecting us to get married. What am I supposed to tell them?"

I level him with a cold, hard stare. "You should've thought of that before you decided to fuck your co-worker. Your *married* co-worker. Does Lucas know?"

"He..." His uneasy gaze flicks between me and a few curious guests lingering nearby. Then he leans closer, his voice turning low and threatening. "You can't do this, Abbey. You *need* me. Don't forget. I've been paying all the bills."

"I'll survive," I declare firmly.

Not giving him the chance to say anything else, I slam the door shut and throw the car into drive, tossing the ring out the window as I speed away.

# THREE

## *Abbey*

Taylor Swift's voice blares from the speakers, and I sing along at the top of my lungs to "We Are Never Ever Getting Back Together". It seems like the perfect anthem for the day I've had.

I have no idea where I am or where I'm going. I can't worry about that right now, though. If I do, reality might come crashing back down on me. I'm not ready to face that just yet.

Instead, I do what I have been since I sped away from Carson a few hours ago — drive aimlessly while listening to a curated playlist of breakup songs to scream in the car, continuing to ignore Carson's frequent calls and texts demanding I return and go through with our planned wedding.

I wish I could say I'm upset he hasn't been faithful.

I'm not.

As horrible as it sounds, I'm more upset about all the plans for my future going up in smoke. I had an idea of what my life would look like by the time I turned thirty — a husband, a house, kids.

A place to belong.

Now I have to start all over again from scratch.

The mere idea has my throat closing up in frustration, but I quickly push it down, especially as the song changes to yet another appropriate breakup song — "Flowers" by Miley Cyrus. I'm so immersed in the song, I barely pay attention to anything else.

Until I register the bleep of a siren.

I look into the rearview mirror, dread tightening my stomach when I see flashing lights behind me. Was I speeding? Did I blow through a stop sign?

I can't be sure of anything right now.

Putting my blinker on, I pull off the main road of what looks like a historic downtown area, certain this day can't get any worse.

But as I come to a stop on a side street and lower the volume of my music, I learn just how wrong I am.

Again.

Instead of a cop casually strolling up to the car and asking for my license and registration, he jumps out of his cruiser, demanding I place my hands on the steering wheel.

Too confused to do anything else, I follow his command. My heart pounds as I watch him cautiously move toward my SUV through the side mirror.

When he draws near and peeks into the car, his brow furrows, obviously surprised to find a woman wearing a wedding dress.

While I'm sure he's encountered his fair share of strange situations in his line of work, I doubt he's ever pulled over a runaway bride.

Or maybe he has.

"How can I help you, Officer?" I tilt my head back to meet his gaze.

He looks to be in his thirties, his attractive face clean shaven, his brown hair well-groomed with a few tattoos peeking out from the arms of his shirt.

"I'm Sergeant Chapman of the county sheriff's department," he states in an authoritative voice. "Can I please see your license and registration?"

"Of course." I'm about to reach for my bag, but hesitate. "Can I take my hands off the steering wheel?"

He gives a curt nod, and I rummage through my bag, grateful I had the wherewithal to grab it in my mad dash to escape my wedding. After retrieving the registration from the glove box, I hand both to the officer.

"I didn't mean to speed. If I *was* speeding. This is probably more information than you want, but if you can't tell, I've had a pretty rough day," I ramble nervously, unable to stop the word vomit from spilling out of my mouth.

"I walked in on my fiancé in a compromising position with my best friend ten minutes before we were supposed to get married. Me and my fiancé. Not me and my best friend. Not that there's anything wrong with that," I add quickly, which earns me a small quirk of his lips. "Anyway, I made a run for it. Since then, I've sort of been blasting breakup songs to help me feel better about this entire fucked up — I mean, messed up situation."

He looks between me and my license, probably trying to make sure it's me, considering my face is now covered with more makeup than I've ever worn and my hair is styled in an intricate updo.

"I didn't pull you over for speeding," he finally announces.

My brows knit together. "Did I run a red light or stop sign?"

"No."

"Then—"

"A few hours ago, this car was reported stolen."

My eyes widen as my heart drops to the pit of my stomach. "S-stolen?"

"Yes, ma'am."

"I… There must be some mistake. My fiancé bought me this car last year." My expression falls. "Or, I suppose, *ex*-fiancé now."

A flash of something genuine flickers in his eyes before he shifts his attention to the car registration. "His name is Carson Dabney?"

"Yes. Which proves this car isn't stolen."

"But it's not yours, either. Since your name isn't on the registration and it's been reported stolen, I can't let you continue driving it unless you have some other proof of ownership."

"I don't think I do." I swallow hard through the ball of frustration tightening in my throat.

Would Carson really do something like this? Would he report the car he bought me as stolen just to spite me for running off on our wedding?

I guess I'm finally seeing his true colors, in all their ugly shades.

"He said it wouldn't matter once we were married."

With a sympathetic look, Sergeant Chapman returns my license. "Unfortunately, without any proof of shared ownership, I'll need to impound it."

"Even if I had permission to use it? Although, I'm not sure he could have anticipated I'd use it to run out on our wedding, but I also didn't anticipate learning he's been cheating on me."

"Listen," he begins, his voice softening. "It's obvious you've had a…difficult day. In my line of work, you learn to determine when someone's lying pretty quickly. I get a feeling you're being honest with me. Unfortunately, I can't let you take off with a car that's been reported stolen by the rightful owner, regardless of how repulsive I think his actions are, given the circumstances. There's nothing I can do about it. I have to impound this car."

I close my eyes, drawing in a deep breath. This entire situation is the icing on an already shitty cake. But if Carson thinks I'll crawl back to him just because he took away my mode of transportation, he'd better think again. I'm stronger than this.

"I'm happy to drive you somewhere if you'd like."

"That's not necessary." Grabbing my bag, I open the door and step onto the pavement, my dress spilling out around me.

"If you change your mind, give me a call." He reaches into the pocket of his uniform and hands me a card. "Just tell dispatch it's an emergency and they'll radio me right away."

"I appreciate it, but I'll be okay. This is all a blessing in disguise. The universe's way of telling me to cut ties with Carson entirely."

"Based on what you've told me, I'd tend to agree. Good luck, Ms. Rhodes."

"Thanks." I give him one last smile, then collect my skirt in my hands to prevent it from dragging as I start up the sidewalk.

As I do, people stop and stare. I can only imagine how ridiculous I look right now in this dress, but I hold my head high, determined to remain positive. I don't need his car. I'll figure out some other way to get to wherever I'm going.

Although, I'm not quite sure where that is. I'm not quite sure where I *can* go, considering I've been living with Carson for the past few years.

In an apartment he owns.

Not only do I not have a car, I also don't have a job or a place to live.

I'm not going to worry about it, though.

I'll figure something out. I always do.

I scan the storefronts of the quaint downtown area that looks like something straight out of a movie, right down to the people happily greeting each other and stopping for a chat. The streets are lined with picturesque lampposts, adding a warm glow to the darkening sky. The scent of sugar and vanilla wafts in the air, and I spy a diner advertising the best chocolate cake in the state.

I'm about to head in its direction before something else catches my attention. A neon sign advertising beer.

Chocolate cake can wait.

Right now, I need something stronger.

# FOUR

## Jude

"For the love of god, we need more help," Dylan whines, shooting me a glare as she hurries behind the bar to pour another round of beers.

The buzz of conversation and laughter surrounds me, a sign that my downtown taproom is once again bustling with customers.

With spring in full bloom, this place has been getting busier and busier, especially with people wanting to enjoy the weather on the outdoor patio that overlooks a play area for kids I put in a few years ago, all to encourage business.

It worked.

A little too well.

Now I'm having trouble hiring enough staff to keep up with demand, which is why my sister's been picking up shifts. Hell, even I'm working the bar when I typically spend my days brewing the beer we serve here at the Wicked Hop.

Lately, however, I have no choice but to forego the time spent brewing so I can lend a hand in the taproom, especially on the weekends.

And this weekend is even busier than the last, a mixture of locals and tourists taking advantage of the warm weather as they enjoy some locally brewed beer.

"I'm working on it, but this isn't just a regular bar," I remind my sister as I pour an IPA. "It's a taproom. Serving only the beer brewed in house. I'd like someone who at least knows the difference between an IPA and a lager."

"At this point, you just need to hire someone, Jude. I'm exhausted from all the hours I've been working here." She swipes at her brow with her arm, pushing her hair behind her ears.

Out of five of us, Dylan's the only blonde.

And the only girl.

Something she still hates, considering she has four older brothers giving any guy she tries to date hell.

"Between this place and helping Hayden with his kids, I barely have any time to myself. Don't get me wrong," she adds quickly. "I'm happy to help, but can you at least *try* to hire more staff? And not require them to provide an essay on how different ingredients used in the fermentation process can affect a beer's flavor. Okay?"

I chuckle. "I'll do my best."

"Good, because if I don't get a day off soon, I'm going to lose it."

"I'm sorry, Dyl."

She's been working non-stop, especially since our oldest brother, Hayden, moved back home after his wife unexpectedly passed away late last year. My mom and Dylan have been helping him with his two kids while he works, which he seems to constantly do. I get he's a doctor and will always need to be on call. It just seems he's working all the time to avoid facing life without his wife.

Then again, I can't blame him. I've been doing the same thing the past several years.

"Why don't you take tomorrow off?" I suggest as I pour another round of beers for a group of tourists at the end of the bar.

"Are you sure?" Dylan sets several full glasses on a tray.

"It's Sunday, so we're only open a few hours anyway."

"I don't want to leave you shorthanded."

"It'll be fine," I assure her. "Just promise me one thing."

"What's that?"

"Don't tell Hayden, or he'll come up with a reason to go into work himself."

"It'll be our little secret." She gives me an exaggerated wink. "You should take a day off once in a while, too, ya know."

"The taproom's closed every Monday."

She narrows her gaze at me. "But you still come in and work in the brewhouse. You need to make time for yourself outside of this place."

"I go to Mom's."

"Because you still use Dad's old brewing system there to experiment."

"And I visit Beckham at the vineyard."

"And Finn at the fire department. Blah blah blah. That's not what I'm talking about, and you know it." She lowers her voice, leaning toward me. "When are you going to move on?"

This isn't the first time we've had this conversation. And I doubt it'll be the last. But it hits harder than usual today, considering what this week represents. It's why I'm working. To forget.

I doubt I will, though.

"You shouldn't keep your table waiting," I say evenly, showing no emotion.

As always.

She blows out a sigh, studying me for a beat. Then she retreats, expertly balancing the tray full of beer as she moves through the busy taproom.

I turn back to the row of taps, snatching the next order as the slip spits out of the machine, and get to work on pouring beer, grateful for the distraction.

Especially today.

A sudden hush falls over the space, catching me off guard, and I look up to see what's going on.

Living in a small town and running a popular hangout, I've seen my fair share of interesting things.

Nothing could have prepared me for the sight of a woman in an extravagant wedding gown pushing her way through the doors of my taproom.

And it's not just any woman, either.

It's her. The bride-to-be from the bachelorette party I stumbled on the other night.

After I left the bar, I immediately regretted sharing my cynical views of love and marriage with a woman who was days away from taking that step.

Now, I feel even worse since I doubt she's here for a celebratory beer.

Several silent moments pass as everyone in the taproom stares at her, myself included. I half expect her to turn around and leave, embarrassed by all the attention.

She doesn't, though.

She holds her head high, determined and unfazed by her situation. One thing is certain. It takes guts to walk into a crowded bar on a Saturday evening wearing a wedding dress that would make Cinderella envious.

"Rough day at the office?" Bernie, one of my regulars, asks as she approaches the vacant chair beside where he's been enjoying a few beers with the other members of the unofficial Sycamore Falls chess club.

"Depends on your definition of rough," she retorts playfully. "If you mean finding out the man you were supposed to marry has been cheating on you with your best friend minutes before your wedding so you ditch him, only for him to report the car he bought you as stolen, taking your only mode of transportation, then yes. It's been a pretty rough day."

"He did?" I press, unable to stop myself.

Her expression falls as she turns to me, clearly annoyed by my presence. Can't say I blame her.

"I guess you were right and I've been wearing rose-colored glasses all along. So congratulations. Feel free to gloat."

"Do you two know each other?" Bernie furrows his bushy gray brow.

"No," I say at the same time as she answers, "Yes."

Bernie eyes me suspiciously, seemingly more inclined to believe this complete stranger than me, someone he's known since the day I was born.

"We met briefly the other night," I explain.

"Is that right?" Bernie looks between the woman and me, obviously intrigued.

"It was quite an enlightening conversation," she says once she's situated on the chair, layers upon layers of fabric flowing out from beneath her. "He shared his opinions on love and marriage, how it's all bullshit, more or less. If I remember correctly, he likened love to a sparkler on the Fourth of July." She looks my way. "All smoke and no substance. Quite the romantic. I'm surprised all the ladies aren't banging down his door."

"Don't pay no mind to Jude," Harold, another member of the chess club, pipes up.

"I don't plan on it." She sits straighter, squaring her shoulders once more. "I didn't have running out on my wedding and losing my car on my bingo card today, but I can make the most of a shitty situation. So I'm going to have a drink, then go down the street and treat myself to a piece of cake, since I've been looking forward to having some since I woke up this morning."

"And after that?" Bernie asks, captivated by her.

He's not the only one, either. Everyone seems to be looking her way. Then again, that could simply be due to the lack of excitement in a small town. Locals will cling onto any big story and talk about it to death, to hell with how it might affect anyone.

"Not sure." She shrugs. "But I'll figure it out. I always do."

"Well, let's get you on the path to figuring it out. Jude, can you get my new friend…" Bernie arches a single brow her way.

"Abbey," she says, picking up on his unspoken question.

"Can you get Abbey something to drink? My treat."

"All we serve here is beer," I tell her curtly. "There's a bar a few miles up the road."

"Do you want me to leave?" she challenges. "I'm not sure the owner of this fine establishment would appreciate learning you've been chasing away paying customers."

"Oh, no," Bernie interjects. "Jude's not—"

"Just giving you an option in case beer isn't your thing," I cut him off before he can finish his statement.

She smooths a hand down her dress. "I'll have you know I quite enjoy a good beer. During my time in the Peace Corps, it was one of the few treats we were able to get our hands on."

I keep my expression even, not wanting her to pick up on my increasing curiosity. I'm not sure what I expected, but based on the enormous rock she wore the other night, plus the wedding dress I can only assume cost five figures, she doesn't come across as the type of woman who'd willingly volunteer two years of her life to work in some third-world country.

"Can I have the imperial?" she asks after scanning the large chalkboard hanging overhead containing my current tap list.

"It's heavy. And strong. It has nearly twelve percent alcohol by volume."

"I'm firing for effect tonight."

With a subtle nod, I turn toward the wall of taps, pouring the honey brown ale into a glass before setting it down in front of her.

"Out with the old, and in with the new." She lifts her glass, her voice filled with determination. "Here's to new beginnings."

I watch as she clinks her beer with Bernie, unsure what to make of this woman who should be devastated but instead is toasting to a new beginning with a man she befriended mere minutes ago.

How can she be so resilient? How can she be smiling?

How can she act as if her world hasn't been flipped upside down?

It both angers and intrigues me, leaving me torn between wanting to find hope in her optimism and wanting to resent her for it.

Because my world was flipped upside down.

And I still feel like I'm drowning every second of every day.

Why isn't she?

# FIVE

## *Jude*

"Are you sure you don't want me to come in tomorrow?" Dylan asks as I arm the security system in the taproom before stepping onto the sidewalk, holding the door for my sister to follow me.

"I'm positive, Dyl." I slide my key into the lock, checking to make sure the door is secure. "Lindsey and Stacy are on the schedule. They can handle it."

"I don't mind helping if you need me."

"I'll be fine. You deserve some time off."

"Thanks."

I give her a nod, then fall into step beside her as we head toward the municipal parking lot a few blocks away. It's in the opposite direction of my townhouse, but I always walk my female employees to their cars after their shift. Granted, not much crime happens in this small town, but I'd rather be safe than sorry, especially where my sister's concerned.

She may be an adult now, but at twenty-five, she's still the baby out of all of us. We may get on each other's nerves, but I'll always look out for her. Hell, I'll look out for all my siblings.

"So tonight was pretty…eventful," Dylan remarks, cutting through the relative silence.

A gentle breeze blows through the crisp night air, a reminder that summer has not yet arrived, even if the temperatures have started to climb during the day.

"How so?" I shove my hands into the pockets of my hoodie, praying she's not about to use this as an opportunity to continue our unfinished conversation from earlier.

"The runaway bride."

We pass a streetlamp, and its golden glow illuminates Dylan's features — her blonde hair pulled back in a messy bun, her green eyes sparkling with amusement. She looks so much like our mom, right down to her petite stature, the rest of us towering over her by over a foot.

"Everyone was talking about her, even after she left. Hell, I'm pretty sure that's why we were busier than normal tonight. Everyone in town wanted to stop by and catch a glimpse of her."

I roll my eyes. "People around here need something better to do than find joy in someone else's misery."

"You can't say you weren't intrigued. You spoke to her for a while. I saw you."

"I asked what she wanted to drink, then I poured her a beer. That was the extent of our interaction," I lie, in no mood to go into detail about the first time I met Abbey.

"You're no fun," Dylan huffs. "I was talking to Mabel when she came in after closing up the diner. Apparently, she stopped by for something to eat and when she tried to pay, none of her cards would work."

I falter in my steps, darting my eyes to my sister. "What?"

"Yeah. Everyone chipped in a few bucks to help her out, but talk about a bad day getting worse."

"I'm sure it doesn't make her feel any better knowing everyone's probably talking about her," I snarl, my words laced with bitterness.

I know what it's like to be the subject of town gossip, everyone seeming to find joy in your misery.

"It's bad enough she's had a shit day, but for everyone to want a front-row seat, too? She's been through enough. Leave the poor girl alone."

"I didn't mean anything by it," Dylan says apologetically. "Hell, I think she showed some serious guts by marching through downtown Sycamore Falls in her wedding dress and acting like it was completely normal. If I were in her shoes, I'd probably hide in a bathroom somewhere and cry until I had no tears left."

"I just hate how some people in this town can be, putting their noses in your business and giving you advice you never asked for."

"Is that why you brushed me off earlier? Because I was putting my nose in your business?"

"You're my sister. You're allowed to put your nose in my business." I playfully nudge her as we come to a stop by her sedan. "Even if it pisses me off."

"It comes from a place of love." She clicks on her key fob to unlock her car.

"I know it does." I wrap her in a tight hug. "Have a good night. And drive safe."

"Always."

Releasing her, I open the door for her, and she ducks in behind the wheel. "Enjoy your day off tomorrow."

"I plan on it." She cranks the engine, then backs out of her spot, giving me one last wave before driving away.

As I walk back through the downtown area, my footsteps echo against the empty streets, the only sounds that of an owl hooting and a frog croaking in the distance. This is my favorite time of day. Most of the downtown shops and restaurants have closed, the town peaceful and quiet now that no one else is around.

At least I *thought* no one else was around.

But as I cut through the park on the way to my townhouse, I notice a lone figure sitting on a bench by the pond. In the dim light, I can make out her familiar silhouette. Even if it was pitch black, I'd know who was sitting there. Hell, I'd know even if she wasn't wearing that damn wedding dress.

Unlike earlier tonight, she's not holding her head high. She's not brimming with optimism, determined to make the best out of a bad situation.

Instead, there's a subtle tremor in her shoulders that has nothing to do with the fact that she's wearing a sleeveless dress in fifty-degree weather.

I don't immediately make a move toward her, telling myself it's not my problem. *She's* not my problem. I can just pretend I didn't see her and continue on my way.

Forget our paths ever crossed.

But I *did* see her.

As guarded and standoffish as I may be, I'm not completely heartless.

How would I feel if Dylan were in Abbey's shoes? If she left her ex and he retaliated by reporting her car as stolen, leaving her stranded in the middle of nowhere? I'd hope someone would help my sister if she were in that position.

I may regret this tomorrow, but after the day Abbey's had, she deserves a little humanity.

So against my better judgment, that's exactly what I decide to do.

Show her some humanity.

# SIX

## *Abbey*

"It's okay," I tell myself, hoping the more I repeat the words, the more I'll believe them. "It'll all be okay. You just need to get through tonight, and then you can figure a way out of this mess. Maybe you'll get lucky and Dad will actually give a shit."

A bitter laugh escapes my throat at the ridiculousness of the suggestion, considering my father hasn't lifted a finger to help me since I turned eighteen. Before that, he made himself out to be the equivalent of Mother Teresa whenever he did anything remotely helpful.

I can't worry about that now, though. I have to remain positive. Otherwise, I'll break. And I refuse to break.

Even if it's taking every ounce of strength I

possess not to curl up into a ball over my current predicament.

Not only did Carson report my car stolen, he did the same for all my debit and credit cards, leaving me penniless. Since my cell phone died hours ago and I left my charger in the car, I'm officially stranded in the middle of nowhere without a place to stay and no means of getting out of here.

At least tonight.

I just have to make it a few more hours. Then everything will be okay. It has to be.

One day, I'll look back on all of this and laugh.

Today is not that day.

A sharp snap of a branch echoes through the stillness, causing me to jolt and turn toward the sound. My breath catches in my throat when I see a figure approaching.

And not just any figure.

*Him.*

Again.

As if it weren't bad enough to come face-to-face with the man who tried to convince me love is bullshit when I walked into the taproom earlier. Now he's here, witnessing me at the lowest I've been in a while. I don't know why I'm surprised. This is just the cherry on the top of an already horrible day.

"Abbey?" Jude raises a single brow as he moves closer. "What are you doing here?"

"Just enjoying the view."

Discreetly wiping away any evidence of tears, I stand and straighten the wedding dress I'd give anything to rip off my body, but it's all I have. Maybe there's a nearby thrift store where I can sell it tomorrow. Make some money and get some other clothes.

"Living in San Francisco, you don't really get to see the stars this clearly."

He nods in contemplation, not saying anything for several long moments as he studies me with a curious expression that makes me uneasy.

"Well, it was nice seeing you again. Have a good night." Gathering up the layers of my dress, I move past him, unsure where I'm going. All I know is he's the last person I want seeing me like this, on the brink of falling apart.

"Where are you staying?"

"Up the road a bit," I reply as I continue retreating.

I refuse to admit my plan was to sleep on the park bench until he showed up.

"I know your card was declined at the diner," he calls out after me.

I come to an abrupt stop and whirl around, a mixture of surprise and frustration brewing inside me. "How did—"

"Small town," he explains as he closes the distance. "News travels fast, whether you want it to or not." He shrugs out of his hoodie and extends it toward me. "Here. Put this on."

I hesitate, eyeing the sweatshirt with suspicion, thinking of the possible ramifications of accepting his help.

"Don't be stubborn. You're obviously cold. I can see the goosebumps on your skin. Just take the damn sweatshirt."

My eyes ping pong between him and the sweatshirt. I want to insist I'll be fine. That I don't need anyone's help, especially his. But he's right. I'm fucking freezing. I'm desperate to feel some sort of comfort, even if it comes in the form of a sweatshirt from a man who probably wouldn't know compassion if it smacked him in the face.

"Thank you." I take the sweatshirt and slide my arms through it. The second I do, warmth envelopes me. Not just from the plush material, but also from the body heat still lingering on it.

A gentle breeze wraps around us, carrying with it his masculine scent, a combination of zesty citrus and earthy sage, melding together to create an intoxicating fragrance that seems to suit him perfectly. Mysterious yet alluring at the same time.

"I'm sorry," he says after a momentary pause, his voice softer than I thought him capable of.

"Excuse me?"

"About the other night. And earlier today. I'm sorry if I did or said anything to make today even more difficult."

I'm not sure what I expected him to say, but it certainly wasn't this.

"I'm fine," I insist, doing my best to remain composed, especially around him.

"Are you?" His deep brown eyes search mine for any hint I'm lying.

And I hate him even more for it.

"Of course." I avoid his gaze, tugging his sweat-shirt closer to my body.

"Then where are you staying tonight?"

"I told you. Up the road a bit."

"Without a credit card?"

I part my lips, struggling to come up with some sort of excuse, but before I can, he cuts me off.

"You were planning to sleep out here tonight, weren't you?"

I shrug. "It's not a big deal. I've been camping before. Hell, I spent two years living in a hut when I was in the Peace Corps. This isn't much different."

"It's a lot different," he grinds out. "For starters, something could happen to you. This may be a small town, but we get a lot of tourists passing through. Someone sees a woman sleeping on a park bench? It's not smart, Abbey, regardless of whether you spent two years living in a goddamn hut."

His chest heaves with frustration, and he draws in a breath in an attempt to calm himself. When he looks at me again, his eyes are soft and full of concern.

"Is there no one you can call?"

"That would require a phone."

His jaw tightens. "Did this prick also turn off your phone?"

"I don't know," I say, my voice wavering slightly.

I hadn't even considered that. God, I hope not. But I have a feeling when I finally find a charger and turn it on, I'll learn he did precisely that.

"It died and my charger is in the car."

He lets out a sigh and runs his fingers through his tousled hair, clearly frustrated by my mere presence. Then he spins suddenly, heading back through the park. "Let's go."

"Go?"

"You can stay with me tonight."

My eyes practically bulge out of their sockets. "What? Why? No. I don't need your charity. Or your pity."

"For fuck's sake, Abbey." He stops walking and spins around, erasing the space between us in three long strides. "You have nowhere to go right now. I'm offering you a roof over your head and a bed. Can you swallow your pride for a minute and let me help you? I get that I was an asshole, and I'm sorry. But don't put your life at risk because you want to prove a point. Otherwise, I'll have no choice but to stay out here with you, and I'd rather sleep in a bed tonight, if it's all the same to you."

His expression softens, the hard edges that have been present every other time I've seen him nowhere to be found. Instead, there's a tenderness I didn't think possible, at least not from him.

"And just so we're clear. I don't pity you," he continues in a gentle voice, his dark eyes awash with sincerity. Something I haven't felt much of lately. "In fact, I think you're probably one of the strongest women I've met in a while. Stubborn as hell, but strong all the same. It takes guts to do what you did, what you're doing. Even after all the shit that asshole's trying to pull. So let me do this for you."

I don't say anything right away, too stunned by his admission and sudden change of demeanor. As much as I want to stand my ground and insist I'm fine, I'm so damn exhausted. Not just physically exhausted from lack of sleep recently, but emotionally exhausted from putting on a façade all day, pretending I'm not one second away from having a complete breakdown.

"Okay," I whisper finally.

"Okay," he repeats. "It's on the other side of the park."

He starts walking, and I follow, falling into step beside him. A comfortable silence stretches between us, broken only by the sound of our footsteps on the pavement and the rustling of my dress.

"Thanks," I say after a few moments. "I really wasn't looking forward to sleeping on a park bench tonight."

"Neither was I. But I would have stayed out here to make sure nothing happened to you."

I steal a glance his way and study his profile. He's definitely attractive, especially under the moonlight. His dark hair falls in waves over his forehead, his brown eyes not giving much away. A day or two of scruff dots his strong jawline and the fabric of his t-shirt clings to his toned physique.

Regardless, I still don't know what to make of him and the wide swings of his demeanor. He's an enigma — mercurial, surprising, confusing. It's almost as if he has to remind himself to act a certain way in order to protect himself.

Maybe I've been wrong about him.

Maybe we're more alike than I originally thought.

# SEVEN

## *Jude*

"This is yours?" Abbey asks as I lead her up the steps and onto my front porch.

With the proximity to downtown, the row of townhomes making up this neighborhood are all designed in a similar style — exposed brick with a white porch and a small patch of grass out front.

"It is." I fish out my keys and insert one into the lock.

"Wow. This is not what I expected. Especially the rose bushes. Unless you hired a landscaper."

"I do all my own yard work."

"That was one of the things I missed when I moved to San Francisco," she muses, following me into the foyer. "No more yard to take care of."

"You enjoy yard work?"

"I do. Or did." Her expression falls slightly, and the furrow in her brow returns, as if deep in thought.

"I'm having trouble picturing you mowing the lawn, if I'm being honest. Then again, I'm also having trouble picturing you living in a hut. It's probably because of the dress."

Abbey laughs, her eyes sparkling with renewed hope. It's a much different look than mere minutes ago when I found her in the park.

"Don't tell me you've never seen anyone mow their lawn in a wedding dress."

"I've never seen anyone walk into my bar wearing one, either. Or walk through the park. Until today."

"There's a first time for everything."

"I guess so." I hold her gaze for a beat before clearing my throat. "Come on. I'll give you the grand tour."

After stepping out of her heels, she follows me into the open concept living and dining area, taking in the moderately-sized space. "This is actually really nice."

"What were you expecting? A shithole?"

"No. I just didn't think you were the type to have potted plants or art hanging on the wall."

I remain silent, not about to tell her my ex-wife decorated this place and, being the masochist I am, I still haven't put it on the market, even when everyone insists I'll never be able to move on when I'm surrounded by horrible memories.

When I'm still stuck in the past.

"I like the whole farmhouse chic vibe you've got going on."

"The guest room is this way," I say evenly, turning from her and heading up the staircase.

I can feel the heat of her stare prickling the back of my neck, as if wanting to ask more questions. Peel back more of my layers. But I have no intention of letting her.

Finally, I hear her footsteps behind me as she makes her way up the stairs.

"Just in here." I head toward one of the rooms off the second-floor landing and flick on the light, revealing a queen-sized bed with a reclaimed wood frame. "It's not the Ritz or Four Seasons."

"It's better than a park bench," she laughs.

"Pretty sure anything would be better than sleeping on a park bench."

"You're probably right." She shifts her gaze to mine, giving me a shy smile that causes a subtle fluttering in my heart.

I trace my eyes over her face, admiring her soft features. It almost feels like this is the first time I'm really seeing her. And not merely because it's the first time we haven't been in a darkened space together. But at this moment, she looks at ease. Like she can finally stop pretending.

"You wouldn't happen to have a spare t-shirt and shorts you could lend me to sleep in, would you?" Her voice breaks through my thoughts. "This is all I have for clothes." She gestures down her frame.

"Right. Of course. One second."

I spin from her and disappear into the room across the landing. A gentle glow illuminates the space from the lamp on my bedside table. Glancing over my shoulder to make sure she's not watching, I hastily smooth the covers over my bed so she doesn't think I'm a total slob. Then I open the dresser, grabbing a t-shirt and a pair of gym shorts before returning to her.

"They'll probably be big on you, but it's better than nothing."

The instant the words leave my mouth, I hear the double meaning. So does Abbey, a smirk crawling on her lips.

"I quite enjoy sleeping in nothing."

She allows her statement to linger in the air between us for what feels like an eternity, her aqua blue eyes dancing with mischief. Then she heads into the guest room.

"But thanks for the clothes."

I can't be entirely sure, considering the layers of fabric she's currently wearing, but it almost looks like she's swaying her hips slightly more than usual.

The second she closes the door, I push out a long breath and run a hand down my face, my mind conjuring all sorts of images of her crawling into bed without wearing a single scrap of clothing.

I quickly push down the thought. That's the

absolute last thing I need to be thinking about with her sleeping across the hall from me. She just ran out on the man she was supposed to marry, for crying out loud. As much of an asshole as I can be on occasion, at least according to my sister, I'm not about to take advantage of someone who's already vulnerable.

Although there's nothing vulnerable about the way she just looked at me.

A voice in my head reminds me she's exactly my type. Witty. Charming. With legs that go on for miles. And the best part? She's just passing through town.

But there's something about Abbey that's different from all the other girls I've sought comfort in over the past few years in the hopes of forgetting, even if only for a little while.

And it confuses me. *She* confuses me.

Which is probably why I've been an ass to her.

"Hey, Jude?" Abbey calls out from the other side of the door with giggle. "It's like that Beatles song," she remarks, then starts to sing the famous song.

"How original," I snip out sarcastically. "I've never had someone make that connection before."

"Right. Sorry." The door opens and Abbey stands in the doorway, still in her wedding dress. "Do you think you can lend me a hand?"

"With what?"

She turns, revealing her back to me, the material sheer with a delicate floral overlay. "There are, like, a thousand buttons on this damn thing and there's no way I can unbutton them myself."

"Right. Sure." With another hard swallow, I approach.

She smooths her blonde tendrils over one shoulder, the motion causing me to catch a whiff of her perfume. Plumeria. Fresh linen. Lavender. It makes me want to bury my face in her hair and never come up for air. Don't even get me started on her skin. Flawless. Smooth. Perfect.

"Is everything okay?"

"Of course." I snap out of my trance and bring my fingers up to the top button.

While there aren't exactly a thousand buttons, there are quite a lot. And they're also ridiculously small, making it a bit of a chore to maneuver each one through the loop.

"They gave me a tool that makes it easier, but I left it behind."

"It's okay." My voice is soft as I finally manage to unclasp the first button. "I don't mind."

For some reason, I like being able to do this for her. Probably because I regret the things I said to her the other night when I wasn't myself. She needs to feel some sort of compassion, even if I'm normally not the kind of guy willing to give that.

As I continue working my way down the line of buttons, they become a little easier. But I still take my time, not wanting to rush this any more than necessary. And with every button, more of her skin is revealed.

I try to be mindful not to brush my fingers against her flesh, but as I reach her waist, the fit becomes slightly tighter, making it more difficult, and I accidentally swipe my hand against her skin. Electricity heats my veins at the same time as a visible shiver rolls through her. Her balance wavers somewhat, causing her to relax her grip on the front of her dress. When she does, I catch a glimpse of the side of her breast, and the dull throbbing consuming me becomes more pronounced.

"Fuck," I hiss, my jaw clenching.

"Everything okay?"

"Yeah. Sorry. I…" I trail off, unsure what to say.

*Sorry I saw the side of your boob, and now I feel like I'm about to explode in my pants like a teenager who's just seen his first pair of tits?*

There's no way in hell I plan on admitting that to her.

"Caught my skin on the button," I finally manage to say.

When she glances over her shoulder and her eyes meet mine, I can see the skepticism within.

"Hope you didn't hurt yourself," she purrs in a seductive tone.

As if catching a glimpse of her breast wasn't bad enough, now she has to respond in that kind of voice?

I consider asking if she wants to kiss it and make it

better, but nothing good can come of that. One of us needs to keep their head on straight. After the day Abbey had, I can't expect it to be her.

"You should be able to get out of your dress now." I step back, trying to calm my racing heart.

And my hardening cock.

"Thanks, Jude."

I don't say anything, just watch as she walks back into the guest room.

And this time, she definitely sways her hips more than usual.

# EIGHT

## *Abbey*

My heavy eyelids flutter open, and I'm greeted by warm sunlight streaming through the blinds of a quaint bedroom. It takes me a moment to remember where I am. Not just because of my unfamiliar surroundings, but because of the unusual silence that engulfs me.

There are no horns honking. No sirens blaring. No cable cars rumbling down the street.

Instead, I'm cocooned in a thick blanket of calm and serenity that makes me question if I'm still dreaming.

As I stretch my sore muscles in the soft bed, memories of the hellish day I had yesterday flood back. Surprisingly, I don't feel as defeated as I did last night.

All because of Jude.

He was the last person I wanted to see during my near breakdown in the park. Hell, he was the last person I expected to go out of his way and help me.

But that's precisely what he did.

I doubt he realizes how much his kind gesture means to me. He may not think much of it, but it gives me hope I'll somehow manage to dig my way out of this hole.

Carefully extricating myself from the warm blankets, I plant my bare feet on the plush area rug beside the bed. The soft fibers tickle my toes as I stand and stretch, my muscles protesting. As I pass the floor-length mirror hanging on the wall by the door, I pause, taking in my appearance. Disheveled strands of blonde hair tumble haphazardly around my makeup-free face, Jude's oversized t-shirt adorning my body, the distressed logo of the Wicked Hop prominent.

I bring the fabric up to my nose and inhale, relishing in the scent. It even smells like him. I shouldn't like it as much as I do, considering I woke up yesterday morning wearing one of Carson's t-shirts. But his never smelled like this. Like grit and man and honesty.

Not wanting to give my ex the satisfaction of thinking about him more than necessary, I open the door and step into the hallway, everything eerily quiet. I assume Jude's probably still sleeping, but when I glance at the door to his bedroom, it's wide open.

Curiosity propels me forward, and I move on light feet toward his room. I shouldn't snoop. Shouldn't even think about invading his privacy like this.

But I'm intrigued by him. Want to know what makes him tick. Why he seems to have this hard outer shell one minute, then acts like a completely different person the next.

I cross the threshold into his room, sunlight illuminating the space, allowing me a better glimpse of it than last night. It's well-appointed, much like the rest of the house. Again, it surprises me.

When I first moved in with Carson, his apartment was undoubtedly masculine — leather furniture, dark wood accents, no hint of anything floral.

That's not the case here.

The walls are painted a soothing light gray with white trim, the navy blue patterned bedspread and floor-to-ceiling curtains the perfect contrast. A framed black-and-white photo of picturesque Lake Tahoe hangs over the bed, with more nature-inspired photos adorning the other walls. There's a subtle touch of femininity in this room that piques my curiosity about Jude even more. Everything about this space gives off the sense that a woman has lived here before, despite there being no trace of one now.

So I move farther into the room, careful not to disturb anything.

The king-sized bed sits in the center, unmade on one side only. The other side is perfect, the duvet and sheets pulled tight, the pillow undisturbed. As if he's accustomed to sleeping only on one side.

A dresser stands against one wall, holding a few scattered items. Just past it, an open closet door reveals a row of shirts and jeans. A stack of books sits on the nightstand by what's obviously his side of the bed.

The nightstand on the opposite side is vacant.

While I'm curious about what book has his attention at the moment, I'm more intrigued by the framed photographs lining a long shelving unit opposite the bed.

Moving toward it, I pick up a picture of three teenage boys, all of them with their arms slung around each other's shoulders. Based on their nearly identical appearance, they must be related.

I grab the next photo, my heart warming at the large family in front of a Christmas tree adorned with glittering ornaments and sparkling lights. Wrapping paper and bows lie scattered at their feet, evidence of a holiday well-celebrated. This photo is clearly more dated than the last, but I have no trouble identifying Jude amongst the five children, who all bear a strong resemblance to each other.

One of the boys is much older than the rest, already a teenager in this photo, while the other three are still elementary school aged. And amongst the four boys is a little girl who can't be more than two years old.

A pang of envy hits me as I continue examining the photos of the obviously happy and close-knit family. I've never experienced this kind of familial bond. I don't see an ounce of irritation or animosity between them. Instead, there's only love and affection.

Not wanting to invade Jude's privacy more than I already have, especially after his hospitality, I turn to leave. But as I do, something catches my eye — the edge of a photo tucked under a ceramic dish. It's probably just another family photo, but I carefully lift the dish anyway.

Like I expected, it's another photo. But this one stops me cold.

A tiny figure floats in a sea of darkness — an ultrasound photo dated a little more than three years ago. Maybe it's a niece or nephew. Given his close relationship with his family, it wouldn't be a far-fetched assumption.

But something tells me it's more than that. The way Jude keeps it tucked away suggests it holds a deeper significance to him.

My heart breaks at what that could be, a chill washing over me.

The silence of the house is suddenly broken by the sound of the front door opening. My pulse skyrockets, a shock of adrenaline shooting through me as I hastily put the photo back, making sure nothing else is out of place. Then I tiptoe out of his room and continue down the staircase, trying to act as if I hadn't just been spying on him.

But my feet catch on the last step, causing me to stumble forward. Just as I brace myself for an embarrassing face plant, two strong hands grip my hips.

"Easy there," Jude's deep voice rumbles in my ear, sending shivers down my spine.

I snap my head up, my eyes tracing over his damp hair and the beads of sweat dotting his brow, making me think he just finished working out.

I shouldn't ogle, but it's impossible when he's less than an inch away.

And he's shirtless.

Broad shoulders narrow into a sculpted chest and defined abs. Don't even get me started on that little V that disappears into his shorts, making me wonder what else is hidden past his waist.

"Are you okay?"

I return my eyes to his, the smirk on his lips giving away that he obviously caught me checking him out.

"Just peachy," I answer, my voice coming out more breathy than I intended.

"Good."

I expect him to release me now that he knows I'm fine.

He doesn't.

Instead, he continues to hold me, neither one of us breaking eye contact.

A surge of electricity courses through my veins,

making me forget everything. My botched wedding. My current predicament. Hell, I even manage to forget about that mysterious ultrasound photo I found mere seconds ago.

Instead, all I can think about is the intensity in Jude's eyes and why the feel of his hands on me seems to ignite something within me.

He takes a slow survey of my body, his gaze lingering on my bare legs before working its way to meet my eyes once more. When he does, I notice something flicker within — curiosity, attraction, longing. Especially when he steals a glance at my lips, as if wondering how they would taste.

Then, with the flip of a switch, his expression suddenly hardens into the same guarded one from our first meeting. He releases me and steps back, creating space between us.

"Help yourself to anything in the fridge. I need to shower and get to work." His tone is even as he pushes past me and up the stairs.

"Thanks," I murmur, but he doesn't look back or acknowledge me. He simply acts as if I'm not even here.

It shouldn't bother me as much as it does. I thought I cracked his tough exterior, especially last night. He was warmer. Softer. Kinder. And the tension that crackled between us as he unbuttoned my dress? I've never felt anything like that, the way my body buzzed to life from the simple swipe of his fingers against my skin.

Or maybe I was so desperate to feel something good after yesterday that I imagined something that's just not there.

Pushing down my confusion, I head into the kitchen, my eyes immediately zeroing in on the one-cup brewer.

Caffeine is definitely needed right now.

With a fresh cup of coffee in my hands, I browse through his well-stocked refrigerator, finding eggs, bacon, as well as some peppers and potatoes I can use to make breakfast potatoes. Then I rummage through his cabinets for a frying pan, surprised at how organized it is, everything exactly where I'd put it if this were my kitchen.

As I chop and dice, I make a list of what I need to do today. My first priority is finding a charger for my phone. Once that's taken care of, I'll call my dad and hope he's willing to pull the stick out of his ass and help me. I could probably reach out to some of my friends from the Peace Corps, but none of them live nearby. My dad's just outside of San Francisco. And he's family. He has to help. Right?

"Smells good."

I startle at the voice, turning to see Jude standing near the island. His hair is damp and slightly disheveled, his body clad in dark jeans and a charcoal gray t-shirt with the logo of the Wicked Hop.

"Want some?" I add the diced potatoes to a pot of boiling water. "It should be ready in about fifteen minutes."

"I have to get to the taproom. We open soon."

"Right. Of course," I laugh nervously, a bit flustered by his presence.

"I picked up a few things for you earlier." He places a shopping bag on the kitchen island. "I wasn't sure what you might need, but I grabbed some clothes, a pair of sneakers, and a charger."

"You didn't have to do that."

"What were you going to wear? Your wedding dress again?"

I shrug. The truth is, I hadn't thought about that, apart from finding a thrift store and selling it.

"I could've just worn this." I gesture to his enormous t-shirt covering my body.

He arches a brow, his gaze briefly dropping to my bare legs. "Most places require pants."

He'd given me shorts, but they were more hassle than they were worth since they kept falling off.

"Well, thanks for all that. I'll be out of your hair soon. Now that I have a charger, I can call my dad and get him to send me some money so I can pay you back."

"Don't worry about it." He waves me off, then grabs a small pad from the counter. "Here's the wi-fi password in case you need it." He hands me the paper containing the network name and password. "You'll be okay?"

I force a smile. "Of course."

Our eyes meet briefly and I can sense there's something more he wants to say. Something meaningful. But he doesn't. Instead, he simply says, "Good luck."

"See ya," I reply softly as I watch him disappear out of the house with a wave goodbye.

# NINE

## *Abbey*

I nervously tap my nails against the cool surface of the kitchen island and stare at the screen of my phone, anxiety filling me. Not because of all the missed calls and texts I received yesterday from Carson, each one becoming more irate.

But because of what I need to do now.

I've put it off as long as I could. I took my time eating breakfast. Then enjoyed a relaxing bath, not getting out until my skin had pruned and the water had become tepid. After that, I got dressed in the clothes Jude bought me, surprised he was able to determine my size with such accuracy, including my bra size.

As much as I don't want to do this, I need money. And a place to live.

Drawing in a deep breath to calm myself, I hit my father's contact and bring my cell up to my ear, listening to it ring. And ring. And ring.

I wouldn't be surprised if he's deliberately ignoring me.

As I'm about to give up and text him, he finally answers.

"Abbey." His voice is cold and distant, lacking the warmth you'd expect between a father and his daughter.

Then again, I never felt like I was part of his family. To him, I'm merely the result of a mistake he made years ago that he's been burdened with since my mother dropped me on his doorstep and informed him I was his problem.

"I thought you'd be on your honeymoon by now."

I don't miss the hint of accusation in his tone. Or maybe it's disinterest.

"Yeah, well, change of plans." I laugh slightly to mask the tremble in my voice.

"What do you mean? Did something happen?"

"You could say that." I swallow hard. "The wedding never happened."

The line goes eerily silent for what feels like an eternity. Then he pushes out a long sigh. "Abbey…"

"Carson was cheating on me. With Maia. I walked in on them together ten minutes before the ceremony was supposed to begin."

"So you just…left?"

This time, I definitely don't miss the accusation in his tone.

"Of course I left."

"With all your guests there?"

"What did you expect me to do? Still marry him?"

"Perhaps there was a better way to handle it other than running out and making a scene," he suggests almost tauntingly. "Then again, you are your mother's daughter. She always had a flair for the dramatics, too."

I clench my jaw, in no mood to get into an argument about my mother with him. She's a sore spot for us both. And he never misses an opportunity to remind me his opinion of me isn't much better than it is of her.

"I'm not calling for your commentary, Graham," I retort sharply, using his first name, as I always do.

Calling him Dad would infer some sort of familial bond. We've never had that. Hell, I've never had that with anyone.

"I need some help."

Another deep sigh sounds over the line. "Let me guess. You'd like that help to come in the form of money."

"Yes," I grit out, hating how this man makes me feel.

"Just like your mother. She only calls when she needs money, too."

"Carson reported the car he gave me as stolen."

"You didn't expect him to let you keep it after you ended things, did you?"

"Honestly, whether I'd be able to keep my car was the last thing I thought about when I walked in on my future husband balls deep in my best friend. I guess I could have interrupted between his grunts and her pleas to fuck her harder."

"No need to get snippy with me, Abbey. I'm on your side."

I roll my eyes, grateful he can't see me.

He loves to claim he's on my side.

He's *never* been on my side.

But I'm not about to delve into how much his actions have affected me.

"Regardless...," I continue, my voice tight with frustration, "I no longer have a car. Carson also canceled all the credit and debit cards tied to our joint accounts."

"You still have your own account, correct?"

"Yes."

"Then use that."

"There's nothing in it." My admission hangs heavy in the air. "After I was laid off last year, Carson didn't want me to stress about finding a job and planning the wedding, so he told me to just focus on the wedding."

"A mistake, as I'm sure you're now realizing."

The tone of his voice makes me feel like I'm one of his employees. Not his own flesh and blood. This is how it's always been with us. Transactional. Devoid of emotion.

"If you want to berate me later for my poor life choices, feel free to get in line. Right now, I'm stuck in a small town in the middle of nowhere with no car, no money, and nowhere to live."

It's a miracle my phone is still on, although I have a feeling that's only so Carson can continue to inundate me with texts. No doubt he'll turn it off in the next few days, too.

"I was hoping you could loan me some money for a flight and an Uber to the airport."

"And after that? Where do you plan on living?"

"I thought I might be able to stay with you and Sharon for a bit. Not long. Just while I figure out what's next. Maybe a week or two, tops."

I hate even asking this. Being back in Graham's house is the last thing I want.

But he's all I have right now. How pathetic is that?

"I'm not sure that's a good idea, Abbey."

And there it is. The answer I knew would come.

"It's not that you're not welcome here. You know you are."

I fight back the sarcastic laugh begging to be set free. I've never been welcome in his home. Even before he kicked me out once I turned eighteen.

"We have a lot going on at the moment. Sharon's got her hands full with Natalie and the twins. Not to mention the new baby on the way."

As if on cue, a loud burst of laughter can be heard in the background, followed by the sound of little feet running and children squealing. The happy family I was never allowed to be a part of.

"With all the upcoming changes, I don't think it's in the kids' best interests to have any additional…disruptions."

"Of course. I wouldn't want to interfere with your perfect life," I bite out.

"It's not like that, Abbey. You're blowing my words out of proportion."

"It's okay. Forget I brought it up. I'll let you get on with your day. I'm sure you have important things to do."

"I'm really sorry, Abbey. But you'll figure things out. You always do."

"Yeah. Sure," I say flatly, pushing down the familiar feelings of rejection and loneliness creeping up inside me. "Thanks for the pep talk."

I end the call before he has a chance to respond.

If I didn't need my phone as badly as I do, I might hurl it across the room.

Instead, I stare blankly ahead, trying to brush off our conversation like it's no big deal. I feel like I did all those years I lived under his roof. Like I'm a guest who's overstayed her welcome.

Closing my eyes, I swallow through the lump in my throat, willing myself not to cry.

Before Carson came into my life with his false

promises of love and stability, this was my reality —
being on my own, living as an outsider. It's what I've
always known.

Just once, I'd like to feel like I belong somewhere.

Like I have a place to call home.

# TEN

## *Jude*

"Table five is still waiting on their IPAs," Lindsey says in a rushed voice as she brushes past me, grabbing a few glasses and pouring her order.

"Can you take care of them for me? I'm backed up."

"And I'm not? Maybe you should call in Dylan."

I steal a glance around the taproom, every table inside taken, as well as most on the patio. The sun streams in through the large windows, bathing the room in light. It seems everyone has decided it's the perfect afternoon to enjoy a few beers.

"She needs a day off. We'll handle it. And if people don't want to wait, they can go somewhere else."

"We need more staff," Lindsey reminds me,

placing her order onto her tray before returning to pour my forgotten IPAs.

"I'm working on it," I reply, turning and setting several beers in front of a group of men around my age, all of them dressed in golf attire.

I take their card and swipe it through the register, then move down the line of thirsty customers awaiting their turn to order.

"What can I get you?" I ask the next group.

But their order fades into the background when the door opens and a woman walks in, a wedding dress draped over her arms.

After I left for work, I wasn't sure if I'd see Abbey again. Part of me didn't want to, not after the way my body reacted to the feel of her skin on mine as I unbuttoned her dress last night. Or the way I had to practically peel my hands off her hips when she fell into me after I returned from my run this morning.

It's a sobering realization.

Sure, I've been with women over the past few years. Probably more than I care to admit. But they were all meaningless. A way to numb the debilitating pain and soul-crushing loss that's consumed me for too long now.

That's not the case with Abbey, and I don't know how to make sense of these feelings stirring inside me, especially after all this time.

"Did you get all that?"

I snap my attention back to the men in front of me. "Sorry. One more time."

One of them rolls their eyes in annoyance, but repeats it, and I get to work on pouring a couple of lagers and a brown ale. After setting the glasses on the bar and swiping their card, I turn my focus to the next group.

"Just give me one second, please. I'll be right with you."

I don't miss their aggravated groans, along with snide remarks that they've already been waiting over ten minutes. But they don't leave. They know my beer is the best around.

I duck out from behind the bar and head toward Abbey. She's wearing the t-shirt and jeans I picked up for her earlier. Her light hair falls to her mid back in gentle waves, not a single lick of makeup on her face.

She looks almost as good as she did this morning wearing just my t-shirt.

"I'm sorry to barge in on you," she says, cutting through my thoughts. "I wanted to say goodbye, and to thank you for everything. The clothes. Phone charger. A place to stay. It means a lot."

"No problem." I cross my arms in front of my chest, and I notice her eyes briefly drift to my biceps. "Were you able to work everything out?"

"More or less."

It doesn't escape my notice that she answers somewhat evasively. I'm about to press for more information, but before I can, Lindsey calls out to me.

"Jude. Break time's over. We're swamped here."

"Right. Sorry. Coming."

"I'll let you get back to work," Abbey offers.

"It's usually not this bad, but I gave my sister the day off and another server called out sick, so I'm shorthanded here. You'll be okay?"

She grits a smile. "I always am. Thanks again."

I give a subtle nod of my head and watch as she makes her way through the taproom and toward the door. A pang squeezes my chest at the idea that I'll never see her again. A strange thought, since she was a stranger mere days ago.

"Jude! Beer!" Lindsey shouts, and I quickly snap my gaze away, rushing back behind the bar.

"Thanks for your patience," I offer the waiting customer. "What would you like?"

He orders a round of IPAs, and I move toward the taps. But when I pull the handle, only sputters of foam come out.

"Shit. I've got to replace the keg."

"Just great," Lindsey replies sarcastically.

"I'll be right back."

Thankfully, I've been doing this long enough that I can change a keg in my sleep.

I weave through the bustling crowd in the taproom, coming to an abrupt stop when I nearly run into someone. I inhale a sharp breath, my eyes flinging wide as I peer down at Abbey.

"What are you doing here? I thought you left."

"I did, but…"

"Yes?"

"You helped me. The least I can do is help you."

I furrow my brow. "What are you talking about?"

"I've bartended before so put me to work. You're obviously short staffed. Let me help."

I blink repeatedly. This is the last thing I expected. Mere seconds ago, I didn't think I'd ever see her again, let alone have her offer to help.

"Jude!" Lindsey yells again, becoming increasingly impatient and frustrated. "I need that tap changed, like, yesterday."

Blowing out a breath, I face Abbey. "Come with me."

She follows me into the back room, practically having to run to keep up.

"You can leave your stuff in my office." I gesture toward the closed door across from us. "And you'll need to put this on." Grabbing a t-shirt from one of the shelves, I toss it at her.

She scrambles to catch it while still clutching that damn wedding dress.

"Give me a sec to switch out this keg, then I'll give you a quick rundown."

I open the door to the walk-in cooler, unhooking the lines from the spent keg before replacing it with a new one. Once everything's connected, I step back into the break room.

But as I do, I stop dead in my tracks. Abbey's mere feet away, clad only in her jeans and a white bra.

The same white bra I bought her this morning.

While I certainly imagined how it would look on her, I didn't think I'd get the chance to see her in it.

I was wrong.

And she looks even better than I imagined, her skin smooth and curves addicting.

As she yanks the fitted t-shirt with my brewery's logo over her head, I avert my gaze, pretending I didn't see anything I wasn't supposed to. Then she faces me.

"Follow me," I order, trying to sound composed despite the spike of desire surging through me.

"Aye aye, captain."

I hurry through the taproom that seems to have gotten even busier in the last couple of minutes, leading Abbey behind the bar. I pull the handle on the IPA and allow the beer to run into a pitcher for a minute.

"It's pretty straightforward. All we serve is beer and it's all on tap. And it's only my beer."

She does a double take. "*Your* beer?"

"This is my taproom. I own the Wicked Hop."

"Oh. I… I thought you just worked here or something." Her eyes scan the row of taps before shifting to the brewhouse that's visible through the windows separating it from the taproom. "I didn't realize you brewed all of it."

"I do." I can't ignore the hint of pride that fills me from the amazement in her voice. But I don't have time to linger on that right now. "Hey, Lindsey," I call out to the tall blonde as she fills her tray with nearly a dozen glasses of beer.

"Yeah?"

"This is Abbey. She's going to help."

Lindsey gives her a nod. "The runaway bride. I heard about you. Welcome aboard."

"Thanks."

"If you can take the patio, Abbey and I will work the inside together."

"You got it."

She carefully lifts her tray off the bar and heads to the doors leading outside.

"Sound good with you? Just do the best you can." I find a paper menu and hand it to her. "All the descriptions are on here. If you have any questions, just interrupt me no matter what I'm doing, okay?"

"Relax, Jude," she says, placing her hand on my arm.

It's supposed to be a soothing, innocent gesture, but the simple feel of her skin against mine ignites something inside me.

"This isn't my first rodeo. I can handle it."

"Okay. Good luck."

She grabs a tray and slips out from behind the bar, flashing me a wink. "Thanks, boss."

# ELEVEN

## *Abbey*

"Here you go." An envelope lands on the table I'm wiping down with a thud.

"What's this?" I ask Jude as I straighten, my muscles sore from running around the taproom all afternoon.

Despite how hectic it was, especially at first, I actually enjoyed myself today. I missed working. Missed feeling useful.

"Your share of this afternoon's tips."

I grab the envelope and open it, my eyes widening at the large stack of cash, mostly twenties.

"Plus your hourly pay. Hope you don't mind it's all cash. Don't tell the IRS." He winks, his lighthearted nature shining through once more.

"Your secret's safe with me, but this isn't necessary." I attempt to hand the envelope back to him.

"You worked your ass off this afternoon, Abbey."

"I didn't help you for the money. I did it because I wanted to repay the favor."

"You did more than repay the favor. I would have been fucked without you, especially when Lindsey had to leave early to take care of her kid. So take the money. You earned it. Plus, I'm sure you could use it right now."

He has a point. This is enough for me to afford a cheap motel room somewhere for a week or two while I figure out my next move.

"Thank you." I stuff the envelope in the back pocket of my jeans.

"Come on. You've earned a beer."

I look around the vacant taproom, not another soul in sight. But there are still dirty glasses on several of the tables. "I haven't finished cleaning yet."

"Leave it. I'll take care of it tomorrow."

"I don't mind. I—"

"Well, *I* could use a beer, and I'd rather not drink alone." He treats me to a hint of a smile, his teeth brilliant against his tan skin. If I thought he was handsome before, he's even sexier now.

"Fine," I eventually relent, unable to say no to that smile. Not to mention, a beer sounds incredible after being on my feet all afternoon.

I follow him toward the bar, my eyes tracing his

every movement as he pulls out a stool for me before hoisting himself over the counter, landing behind it with ease.

"I would have laughed my ass off if you fell," I tease as I climb onto the stool, my feet sighing with relief.

"I've done that more times than I can count."

"Fall or jump over the bar?" I lift a playful brow.

"Both." He grabs a clean glass from the counter. "What'll it be? Imperial again like last night?"

I shift my eyes to the large board overhead, even though I have the tap list memorized after working the past few hours.

As I poured the various beers people ordered, I made a point to read up on each of them. The IPAs seem to be the most popular, but I don't want to have something everyone else has.

"What's *your* favorite?" I ask.

"They're all my favorite. I wouldn't sell them if I didn't like them." He tilts his head and studies me. "Want to try something new?"

"Why? So I can be your guinea pig?"

"That's what my brothers and sister are for. Follow me."

With ease, he jumps back over the counter and leads me toward the back hallway. A wall of glass separates a large space filled with several steel vats in varying sizes.

Approaching a door off to the side, he punches in a code before holding it open for me.

"I'm guessing this is where the magic happens," I remark as I walk inside.

"More or less."

"This is impressive." I take in my sterile surroundings, everything gleaming and spotless under the fluorescent lights. "I wouldn't even know what any of this stuff is for."

"It took me a while to learn, too." He chuckles as he leads me toward a walk-in cooler.

But unlike the one behind the bar that's filled with kegs, this one is lined with rows and rows of bottles, each adorned with the Wicked Hop logo.

"This is a new Vienna lager I've been playing around with," he explains as he grabs two bottles from a six-pack. "I'm planning a limited release to see how it's received."

With a flick of his wrist, he pops the top off and hands one to me.

"Cheers."

"Cheers," I echo, touching my beer to his before taking a sip.

The flavor is unlike any beer I've had before — rich and robust with layers of complexity I can't quite put my finger on. But what's even more remarkable than the taste is the fact that Jude brewed this himself. This isn't just some random hobby or amateur attempt at home brewing. This is a masterful creation that was crafted by his own hands in this very room.

"What do you think?"

"It's incredible, Jude. All of this…"

I'm filled with awe and admiration as I look around the brewhouse again, seeing Jude in a whole new light.

"How did you get into this?"

He leans against a steel table set against the wall, and I join him. "My dad, actually."

"Really?"

He nods and sips his beer. I do the same, trying to imagine what it must have been like for Jude to share this passion with his father.

I wouldn't know what that's like.

"He also brewed his own beer. Not on this level." He gestures at the professional-grade equipment. "But he still had a pretty decent setup. Even turned the garage into a makeshift bar. Whenever he had a fresh brew ready, locals would come over. Dad never charged, but you always knew when he had something new because he'd illuminate a neon sign in the window of the garage that said BEER. He found it at some estate sale and my mom thought he'd lost his mind."

He laughs to himself, a glint of nostalgia making his eyes shine. It's obvious from the affection in his tone and expression that he adores his father. But within that affection, there's a hint of sadness, making me think he may no longer be around.

"Is it the same sign hanging out front?" I ask, recalling seeing a sign exactly as he described in the front window of this taproom. Hell, it was what caught my attention yesterday after I was pulled over.

"It is." He peers into the distance for several long seconds before clearing his throat. "After a few years of brewing his own beer, he decided he needed a better name than just Ryan's Beer. Ryan was my dad's name," he explains.

"I see."

"Since he's originally from Boston, he decided to name it—"

"The Wicked Hop," I finish.

"Exactly."

He takes another long sip of beer, his throat working as he swallows. There's something oddly sexy about the way he casually leans against the table and savors his own creation. With every minute I spend in his presence, I find myself drawn to him in ways I never expected, especially after only knowing him a short period of time.

"He had ALS and died my senior year of high school," he announces. "Two days before I was supposed to graduate."

"Oh, Jude…"

I shake my head, searching for something appropriate to say. A part of me is surprised by the vulnerability he's currently showing me. Then again, maybe my assessment of him last night is right. He may have a hard exterior, but he's soft on the inside. You just have to find a way past his tough outer shell first.

"That summer, I found his notebook with different recipes and decided to try my hand at making a batch. Even though he let me help him brew beer a few times, I had no idea what I was doing. I still wanted to try." He laughs slightly and glances at me. "You'll probably think this sounds ridiculous, but I swear I felt my dad's presence with me."

"I think that's sweet." I continue sipping on the beer, each swallow becoming more flavorful as I peel back more of his layers.

"To this day, whenever I'm making beer, whether in here or my mom's garage, I feel him. Hell, sometimes I come in here just to talk to him. Or to the garage at my mom's."

"Is all his brewing equipment still there?"

"It is. It's actually where I do my test runs."

I can't stop the grin from spreading on my lips. "I love that story. It's…perfect."

"Thanks."

"What about college?" I ask, wanting to learn everything I can about him while he's in a sharing mood. There's no knowing when he'll shut down.

From my experience, he can go from hot to cold in a heartbeat.

"I dropped out of college. Well, technically, I got kicked out."

My eyebrows shoot up in surprise. "For what?"

He shrugs as a sly smile curves the corner of his mouth, causing the most adorable dimples to appear.

As if he weren't attractive enough before, now he has to have dimples?

It gives him a boyish charm I find nearly impossible to resist.

"For brewing beer on campus."

I throw my head back and laugh. "Did you really?"

"That, and I'd pretty much stopped going to class. My beer had started to grow in popularity. Why waste time sitting in class when I could be brewing, bottling, and distributing my own beer?"

"How did you end up with all of this?" I wave my hand at my surroundings.

"A lot of blood, sweat, and tears." He takes another swig of beer. "But I knew this was what I wanted to do. The idea of sitting in a classroom or in an office never appealed to me. I moved back in with my mom and worked my ass off to increase production. Then I started reaching out to every taproom, restaurant, and bar within a two-hundred-mile radius to see if they'd want to carry my label. It was tough at first, but eventually, I had sufficient demand to warrant opening my own taproom."

"That's incredible." I laugh under my breath. "I feel like a failure next to you."

"You're not a failure. You were in the Peace Corps, for crying out loud. I was definitely impressed when I learned that."

I shrug, averting my gaze. "I just wanted to do something worthwhile."

"What did you do while you were in the Peace Corps?" He inched toward me, genuine curiosity etched on his face.

"My focus was on clean water. In a lot of less developed countries, clean water isn't a guarantee, so my time there was spent educating the locals on its importance and helping to develop systems for them to be able to access it. Especially women, since they're typically the ones responsible for fetching water for their families."

He studies me for a moment, taking in every word as if truly interested. "Sounds like it's something you're passionate about."

"I think everyone should have access to basic necessities."

"And after the Peace Corps? What did you do?"

I take a sip from my beer. "Came back to the States and worked for a nonprofit in a similar field. But then I was laid off late last year due to budget cuts. With the wedding coming up, Carson suggested I focus on planning that instead of stressing over finding and starting a new job."

"I see," he replies evenly as another protracted silence stretches between us. "Well, I'm sure you'll find something. You're obviously passionate about what you do."

"I hope you're right," I murmur.

I may have a few years of experience, but it's nothing compared to people who have been doing this for decades. Nonprofit jobs are hard enough to come by as it is. But I need to remain positive. Need to remain hopeful. Otherwise, what's the point?

"Well, I won't keep you here any longer," Jude says, pushing off the table. "I'm sure you want to get on the road to your next destination before it gets too late."

"Of course." I tip back my bottle and finish my beer.

After tossing our bottles into the recycling bin, I follow Jude through a different door, this one leading into his office. I grab my bag and wedding dress, then remember I'm wearing a different shirt.

"Do you want this back?" I ask, gesturing to my shirt.

"Keep it." He waves a dismissive hand. "I've got plenty. That way, you'll have a souvenir of your time here. Although, I doubt this is something you'll want to remember."

"Yesterday, not so much. But today?" I shrug, meeting his eyes. "I'd like to remember today."

Jude's expression softens and a hint of warmth flickers in his eyes as they meet mine. "I'd like to remember today, too."

# TWELVE

## *Jude*

"I'll wait with you," I announce when I step onto the sidewalk with Abbey after locking up the taproom.

The last remnants of sunlight glow on the horizon, painting the sky a beautiful mixture of pinks, blues, and purples. The town is already closing up, despite it not yet being eight o'clock. Most storefronts are dark, except for the nearby diner and pizza parlor, both of which will soon close, as well.

When I moved back here after dropping out of college, I worried I'd made a mistake. Worried I'd miss the fast-paced atmosphere of LA. Now, I can't imagine living anywhere else. While I don't love everything about living in a small town, especially the rumors and gossip, I like the slower pace of life here.

"Wait with me?" Abbey gives me a quizzical look. "What do you—"

"You're going to order an Uber, right?"

"I, uh… Right."

I study her closely as she rummages through her bag. A nagging feeling forms in my gut that she wasn't completely honest with me earlier when she said she worked everything out. And that feeling gets even stronger when I steal a glimpse of her phone screen as she pulls it out of her bag — a text message prominent from someone named Graham.

GRAHAM:

I'm sorry if I upset you earlier when I said I couldn't help, but it's really for the best if you land on your own two feet instead of depending on someone else.

Who the fuck is Graham? And why does it look like Abbey's about to scream in response to his message?

"Is everything okay?" I ask, closing the distance between us. As I do, the breeze kicks up her floral scent, and I draw in a deep breath, savoring her sweet fragrance.

"Of course." She grits a smile, as she moves away, as if purposefully not wanting me to see her screen. Her brows pull together, uncertainty flashing in her expression.

Which only increases my suspicion, my protective instincts kicking in.

"Abbey?"

She darts her head up. "Yeah?"

"You *do* have somewhere to stay tonight, right?" I ask firmly, planting my feet wide apart. "And a way to get there?"

"I, uh…" She chews on her bottom lip to hide the subtle tremble.

"When you came to say goodbye earlier, where were you planning to go?" I ask firmly.

She parts her lips, but before she can answer, I interrupt, "And don't lie. I'll know."

"How? You barely know me."

"The vein in your forehead. It pops whenever you're trying to hide something. Or, at least, when you try to pretend you're okay even though you're anything but." I step toward her. "So I'm going to ask again. Where were you planning to go after leaving the taproom earlier today?"

"The park," she answers in a strained voice.

"The park?" I shoot back incredulously.

"Not the whole time. I planned on hitting up the coffee shop, too. At least until they kicked me out for not buying anything. I had hoped to go to a thrift shop to sell this…" She lifts her dress. "But they're closed on Sundays."

"I thought you were going to call your dad?" I give her a quizzical look.

"I did." She raises her head defiantly, and it reminds me of how she acted last night when I found her in the park.

When she didn't want anyone to see her on the verge of having a breakdown.

"Then why—"

"I don't have the same relationship with my dad that you did, Jude," she shoots back, her voice shaking. "Mine couldn't even be bothered to show up for what was supposed to be my wedding, so I'm not surprised he refused to help when I called him."

"Abbey…," I exhale, trying to wrap my head around this.

I may have experienced my fair share of bad shit, but I never questioned my family's love and support. Most days, it's the only thing that gets me through.

"It's okay," she continues. "I'm used to it. But thanks to you, I have some money, so I'll just find a cheap motel, preferably within walking distance." She starts typing on her phone again. "Here's one. Only five miles away. Bella Vista Village. That sounds nice."

I snatch her phone out of her hand. "You are *not* staying at the BV."

"The BV?"

"Trust me. It's a dump. They tend to rent rooms by the hour, if you catch my drift."

"I can't exactly afford the Ritz right now, Jude," she shouts, throwing her hands up in frustration, her voice echoing against the brick buildings. "So unless you have a better option, the BV is my only goddamn choice. I—"

"You can stay with me," I blurt out before I can stop myself. "Hell, you can work for me, too."

She sucks in a breath, momentarily speechless, as if trying to make sense out of my offer.

I'm trying to make sense of it, too.

"What did you say?" she asks finally, cutting through the heavy silence.

I can take it back right now. Let her go on her way. If she wants to stay at the BV, so be it. But for reasons I can't quite explain, I don't.

"It's not as fulfilling as developing ways for people to get clean water." I hand her phone back to her. "But it's a way for you to get back on your feet. You saw it for yourself. I need more staff. And with the weather getting warmer, it's only going to get busier. I used to be able to spend most of my time brewing beer. Now, I need to go in early if I want to get anything done because of how busy the taproom's gotten. Don't get me wrong, I'm grateful, but I need help."

"You're offering me a job *and* a place to live?" she asks slowly, as if convinced she misheard.

As if she's so used to nothing in her life going right that she doesn't know how to react when something does.

"There's no way in hell I'm going to let you stay at

the BV, Abbey," I respond with determination. "That's worse than the park bench. We used to joke about it in high school. Go to the BV. Come home with an STD."

"It's that bad?"

"Worse."

She presses her lips into a tight line, shaking her head in confusion. "Why are you doing all of this for me? The job? The room? The clothes?" Her eyes search mine. "I don't get you, Jude. You're cold one minute, then warm the next."

I blow out a breath and run my fingers through my hair. "Truth be told, I don't get me most of the time, either. And while I probably didn't make the best first impression, I'm usually a pretty decent guy." I give her what I hope to be an apologetic smile. "You just caught me on a bad day."

"I don't—"

"Take the job, Abbey," I plead. "I'm desperate. I really need some good help. And I'd like to think your boss isn't too much of an asshole, despite first impressions."

"And the room?"

"What about it?"

"Are you sure you want me moving in? That I won't be interfering with your lifestyle or anything?" Her words are cautious, and I know what she's asking without having to come right out and say it.

She's worried having a roommate will interfere with my dating life.

But there is no dating life.

There never will be again.

"It's fine. I'm rarely there as it is."

"And the rent?"

"What do you mean?"

"How much do you want for rent?"

"Don't worry about paying rent. Just focus on getting back on your feet."

She looks off into the distance, worrying her bottom lip once more. Finally, after what feels like an eternity, she nods. "Okay. But only until I get back on my feet." Shifting her wedding dress so it's draped over one arm, she thrusts her hand out toward me.

"Deal," I tell her.

As I take her hand in mine, I can't help but feel a spark of electricity travel down my spine from the warmth of her skin against mine. It makes me want to hold on tighter, but I force myself to let go and create some space between us.

"What do you say we grab a pizza before heading home?"

"Sounds good to me," she responds, playfully nudging me with her shoulder. "Roomie."

Placing my hand on the small of her back, I guide her down the street toward the only pizza place in town, praying I didn't just make a colossal mistake by letting her move in with me.

# THIRTEEN

## *Jude*

"I 'm impressed," Dylan remarks, breezing into the taproom Tuesday afternoon as I wipe down the glasses that just came out of the dishwasher.

"What are you talking about?" I ask with a furrowed brow. "I polish glasses all the time."

"Not that. I told you to hire someone, and the next time I come in, there's already someone new working?" She nods toward the patio where Abbey's currently talking animatedly with a few of the guys from the local repair shop, as if they're old friends instead of strangers.

That seems to be the effect she has on people. I noticed it the night she walked in wearing that wedding dress. And I've seen it again today as I've watched her work. People are drawn to her.

Hell, *I'm* drawn to her. It's part of the reason I've been hanging out here instead of in the brewhouse, even though there are dozens of things needing my attention. I tell myself I'm just being a good boss and making sure she doesn't run into any problems on her first official day here.

In reality, it's because I like being able to look her way every few seconds.

"Who is she?" Dylan asks, ducking underneath the bar to store her purse in its usual hiding spot.

"Just a new employee," I respond dismissively.

"Gee, really? I didn't figure that out," she shoots back sarcastically. "Who is she? She's not a local."

"She's not."

She parts her lips, about to continue her inquisition, but I cut her off before she can.

"How were Presley and Jeremiah?"

Dylan studies me for a protracted beat, her piercing green eyes analyzing everything I do. I expect her to accuse me of purposefully changing the subject. I don't know why I'm not being forthcoming with her. It's not like she won't eventually find out who Abbey is.

But she's not just my new employee. She's also my new roommate. There's no doubt in my mind she'll overthink what that means. It doesn't mean anything.

"Presley's doing a little better," she finally answers as she washes her hands. "Some kids at school still make fun of her because she won't talk."

"Fucking assholes," I mutter, unable to stop myself.

I may not have spent much time with my niece and nephew before they moved here, but I feel fiercely protective of them as they attempt to adjust to life without their mom.

All because some asshole teenager just couldn't wait a few more minutes to send a text.

It's no wonder she hasn't spoken since. I'm not sure I'd want to talk after going through something like that at only six years old.

Hell, I didn't want to talk after going through something similar at my current age. Still don't.

"She's making friends, though," Dylan pipes up, pulling out a cutting board and getting to work on slicing some oranges used to garnish one of my lighter brews. "A few of the girls in class play with her at recess. According to her teacher, they play the 'quiet' game."

"The 'quiet' game?"

"Apparently, they can only communicate using body language. The first person who talks loses." She flashes me a mischievous smile. "Presley is the reigning champion."

"Of course she is," I say with a chuckle. "I'm glad she's adjusting, all things considered."

"Me, too," she answers affectionately, the love she has for her niece and nephew apparent.

That's the one thing I'll never take for granted.

My siblings may get on my nerves, but they're always there for each other when it counts. Especially Dylan.

In many ways, she's the glue that holds us together, even if she's the youngest.

She not only helps me out at the taproom whenever I need it, she's been practically raising Presley and Jeremiah for our oldest brother, Hayden. She's done more than most people would in her position. All the more reason I'm glad I hired Abbey. My sister deserves to take some time for herself. Pursue her own passion, whatever that may be.

"Now that I've answered *your* question, it's time you answer mine. Who's the new girl? And don't give me some lame answer about her being a new employee."

I inwardly groan as I pull more glassware out of the dishwasher. I should have known Dylan wouldn't let it go. She can be like a dog with a bone. She won't let up until she's gotten to the juicy bit.

"Her name's Abbey," I finally relent, but don't look my sister directly in the eye, keeping my focus on polishing the glasses. "And you're right. She's not local, but she needed a job and, as you've reminded me time and again, I need more staff. So there you go." I run the cloth against the glass a touch harder than necessary. "More staff."

"Abbey? Why does that name…" She trails off and sucks in a sharp breath. "Is that the runaway bride?"

I look in Dylan's direction, about to remind her that one awful incident doesn't define who she is. But before I can, Abbey's voice cuts in.

"Guilty as charged," she sings, an air of confidence about her as she floats toward the serving station. "Abbey Rhodes." She extends her hand toward my sister, and they shake.

"Dylan Lawrence."

Abbey's eyes widen. "You're Jude's sister!"

"The one and only. Literally. Out of five kids, I'm the only girl. You can imagine what my dating life is like with four older brothers. Four *overbearing* older brothers. Especially this one." She hooks a thumb my way.

I lean against the counter and cross my arms in front of my chest, enjoying the lull before the post-work rush. "In my defense, some of the guys you dated were assholes, Dyl."

"No worse than you, my darling brother," she teases before returning her attention to Abbey. "How are you settling in?"

"Great. The people in town here have been very welcoming. Especially Jude. If it weren't for him, I'm not sure what I would have done."

"Is that right?" Dylan floats her curious eyes from Abbey to me, as if trying to unravel a puzzle. But there's no puzzle to unravel. Abbey needed help. End of story.

"Between the job and his spare room, he's been a life saver," Abbey continues.

Dylan's smirk grows wider with every piece of information she shares. It's not the fact that she's working here and staying in my spare room that has my sister acting this way. It's the fact that I obviously tried to keep it from her. Why, I'm still not sure.

"So you're staying in his spare room." Although her statement is in response to Abbey, I can tell it's actually directed at me.

"Just until I find somewhere else to live, so if you hear of anyone who's looking for a roommate, let me know."

"I'll be sure to keep that in mind," Dylan responds with a sly grin in my direction, which I return by shooting daggers at her, the two of us engaged in a silent argument, much like we often did as kids when we didn't want our parents to yell at us for fighting again.

Some things never change.

"Thanks." Abbey looks between Dylan and me with confusion, then grabs the two beers I just poured for her. "Great to meet you, Dylan."

"Oh, it is absolutely fantastic to meet you, Abbey."

The crease in her brow deepens in response to Dylan's tone, but she doesn't question it, turning and heading out to the patio instead.

"So…" Dylan sidles up beside me and leans against the stainless steel counter once we're alone.

I ignore my sister, continuing to polish each piece of glassware with focus and precision, as if it's the most important task on my to-do list. Pretending I'm too busy to talk is my only defense against my sister's incessant nagging, albeit a weak one.

"You not only hired the runaway bride, but you're *living* together?" She lets out a low whistle. "Talk about moving fast."

"Stop being so damn dramatic, Dylan. It's not like that."

I place the freshly polished glass onto the shelf and grab a new one, sneaking a quick glance toward the patio.

"From where I'm standing, it kind of looks like that."

I snap my head forward again. "I'm just helping her out. As if her ex cheating on her isn't bad enough, when she called her father for help, he refused."

"Really?"

"Wouldn't let her stay with him or send money."

Dylan's jaw drops and she shakes her head. "Wow. That's… What a douche."

"Tell me about it. Can you imagine if you were stranded in the middle of nowhere with no money after learning the man you were supposed to marry has been cheating on you, and when you called me for help, I essentially said 'sucks to be you but I'm sure you'll figure it out.'"

"Pretty sure I'd be bailing all of you out of jail for murdering my ex. Provided I didn't get to him first."

A small laugh escapes my throat. "You probably would be."

We may be joking, but there's no doubt in my mind I'd do whatever it takes to protect my little sister. The idea of her going through something similar played a big part in why I offered to help Abbey in the first place. I couldn't stand the thought of my sister being in Abbey's shoes with no one to turn to.

"I'm proud of you, Jude. This could be good for you. Could be exactly what you need to move on."

"What are you talking about?"

Dylan pauses in the midst of slicing an orange, pinning me with a knowing look. "I'm talking about finally moving on from Krista." She swallows hard. "And—"

"Don't," I bark out, my voice reverberating against the walls, drowning out the rock music being piped in through the speakers.

A few of the patrons glance our way, and I give them an apologetic look before returning my attention to the glassware.

"I've moved on," I tell my sister, although my voice lacks any conviction.

"Sure you have," she snips back, her words laced

with disbelief. "That's why you still live in the same damn house. It's been three years, Jude."

"So you just want me to forget?" I bite out, trying to keep my voice low, even as my emotions threaten to boil over. "Do you tell Presley the same thing? Tell her she just needs to get over losing the most important person in her fucking life?"

"I'd never ask her or you to forget. It's like asking the sun not to rise or the rivers to stop flowing. It won't happen."

She sets the knife on the cutting board and steps toward me, giving my tense forearm a reassuring squeeze.

"But like I tell Presley… Her mom would want her to have the best life. The same goes for you, Jude. And maybe this is exactly what you need so you can finally have that."

# FOURTEEN

## *Abbey*

The soft hum of music fills the room as I flow from one yoga pose to the next, solely focused on my breath and maintaining balance and harmony.

After I ran out on Carson, I never thought I'd feel centered and at peace again.

Now, I feel more at peace than I have in a long time, thanks to Jude.

A smile tugs at my lips at the mere thought of him. Over the past few weeks, I've seen a completely different side of him than the man I first met on the night of my bachelorette party.

Granted, his grumpy side makes an appearance on occasion, but I'd like to think I've learned the secret to cracking through that tough outer shell.

And when I do, there's nothing better than his laugh. And don't get me started on those dimples.

As I transition into a reverse warrior pose, the doorbell interrupts the peaceful serenity of the townhouse. Assuming it's just a delivery, I remain in the lunge position with one arm extended over my head and the other along my leg, maintaining steady breaths.

Then a feminine voice breaks through.

"Abbey? Are you in there? It's Danielle Lawrence. Jude's mom. I know he's out for a run, so I figured now would be the perfect time to drop by."

I straighten, nervous butterflies taking flight in my stomach over the prospect of meeting Jude's mom. But I have nothing to be nervous about. It's not like I'm *dating* him or anything. I just work for and live with him. Temporarily.

That's it.

"I brought banana bread and blueberry scones," she sings.

"Coming," I call out, quickly rolling up my yoga mat and propping it against the wall.

After turning off the music on my phone, I hurry toward the front door, pausing by the entryway mirror to check my appearance. My complexion is slightly flushed, my blonde curls pulled back into a messy bun on the top of my head. Not exactly presentable, but it'll have to do on such short notice.

Drawing in a breath, I turn to the door and open it to reveal a petite woman with a plate of baked goods in her hands. She looks like an older version of Dylan — blonde hair, green eyes, and a heartwarming smile.

"I hope I'm not interrupting." She scans my attire — tight fitting tank top and slim black yoga pants. "I thought I'd drop by to meet Jude's new roommate and bring you a little something."

"You're not interrupting at all. I was just doing some yoga, but I'd much rather eat. Come on in."

I step aside, and the smell of freshly baked bread fills the air as she walks inside.

"I'd much rather eat than do yoga, too. My body doesn't bend that way anymore."

I laugh politely and follow her into the kitchen. "Would you like some coffee, Mrs. Lawrence?"

"If it's not any trouble. And please. Call me Danielle."

"Okay, Danielle."

I head toward the one-cup brewer and prepare a few cups while she takes a seat at the bistro table, unwrapping the plate of goodies. Once I'm done, I place two mugs onto the table, along with milk and a variety of sweeteners.

"How are you liking Sycamore Falls so far?" she asks after preparing her coffee and taking a sip, her eyes sparkling with genuine interest.

"It's definitely quieter than what I'm used to in San Francisco, but it's nice. Everyone has been so welcoming and kind."

"My son included?" She arches a brow, obviously well aware of how he can be.

"Your son included," I assure her. "I don't know what I would have done if he didn't help me. Not only offering me a job, but a place to stay? There's a good person hidden underneath that tough exterior."

"That's my Jude. He has a heart of gold." A nostalgic gleam sparkles in her eyes as she gazes off into the distance. "When he was little, he found a stray dog on the side of the road and begged us to keep it, even though we already had two dogs. Said it was his duty to help. Even attempted to build a doghouse — by himself, mind you — without telling anyone. We came outside, and there he was, hammering away. He couldn't have been more than seven."

"That must've been something to see," I remark, wanting her to tell me everything Jude's ever done so I can get a deeper understanding of who he is.

While we've been living and working together, we haven't had many deep conversations. Not since the first day I helped out at the taproom. Instead, our interactions have been mostly work-related, supplies that need to be ordered or other issues that arise.

"It was. He's always had a good heart. A kind soul," Danielle says, her voice full of affection. "But he's had his fair share of heartbreak, too. More heart-break than anyone should have to suffer."

The words linger between us, and I'm reminded of the ultrasound photo I found in his room. While I don't feel right asking her about it directly, considering I discovered it when I was snooping, maybe I can get her to share more about Jude's past without prying too much.

But before I have a chance, the front door opens and heavy footsteps move through the townhouse before coming to a stop. I shift my eyes up, my cheeks heating at the sight of Jude, shirtless and sweaty from his run, muscles taut, skin glistening. He's all hard lines and raw intensity, and I have to force myself to look away. I can only hope Danielle doesn't notice the flush creeping up my face.

Hope *Jude* doesn't, either.

"Mom, what are you doing here?"

"Is that any way to greet the woman who endured over twenty-four hours of labor to bring you into this world?" she retorts playfully, unfazed by his somewhat gruff tone. "I came to meet your new roommate. Brought some of my famous banana bread and blue-berry scones."

"They're quite delicious," I offer around a mouthful of scone.

"You shouldn't just come over unannounced," he says evenly. "Abbey may have things she needs to do."

"I don't mind. Your mom's been telling me all about how you were as a little boy."

"Don't believe a word out of her mouth." He heads into the kitchen and grabs a bottle of water from the refrigerator. I have to purposefully avoid gawking at him as he takes a sip. He looks like a walking advertisement for a sports drink company.

"You should come to Second Sunday tomorrow evening," Danielle suggests to me.

"Second Sunday?" I furrow my brow, taking another sip of my coffee.

"It's a family tradition," she explains. "We all get together for a big dinner the second Sunday of every month."

"I wouldn't want to intrude on your family time."

"Nonsense." She covers my hand with hers. "The more the merrier. I'd love to have you."

"I'm sure she doesn't want to spend her Sunday night dealing with our family," Jude says, rubbing the back of his neck.

"It sounds nice, actually." I shift my attention back to Danielle. "I'd love to go. Thank you for including me."

"Wonderful!" Danielle beams, clearly pleased. "Jude can drive you." When she looks his way and smirks, something passes between them. It reminds me of the looks he's shared with Dylan at the bar, as if they're having entire conversations without uttering a single word.

I suppose when you're as tight-knit of a family as they appear to be, you can do that.

"Well, then…" Danielle cuts through the silence, pushing back from the table and standing. "I'll get out of your hair. I'll see you both tomorrow."

"Looking forward to it," I say as I stand.

"It was lovely to meet you, Abbey." She wraps me in a hug, catching me off guard. I've never experienced this level of affection from a complete stranger before.

Hell, I've never even experienced this level of affection from my own family, if you can even consider my parents family.

"You, too," I manage to say, hiding the emotion in my voice.

She pulls back, giving me a once over before dropping her hold on me and moving toward Jude.

"Love you, Jude."

"Love you, too, Ma." He leans down and brushes a soft kiss to her cheek.

Once the door closes behind her, Jude shifts his gaze toward me.

"You really don't have to come tomorrow if you don't want to," he says softly. "My mom can be a bit pushy. I don't want you to feel pressured into doing something you're not comfortable with. You're not required to come just because you live here."

"Do you not want me there?" I shift my weight, crossing my arms in front of my chest. I notice his eyes briefly dip to my cleavage before returning to my face.

"I just don't want you to feel obligated. That's all."

"Well, I want to come. I mean, go. I'd like to go."

"Okay." He nods, his gaze lingering on me a little longer than normal before he finally turns and disappears up the stairs.

# FIFTEEN

## *Jude*

"I see you invited the runaway bride to Second Sunday," Finn remarks, plopping down beside me as I relax on the back patio of my parents' house.

"I didn't invite her." I take a long swallow of my beer and turn toward my brother. "That was all Mom's doing. I walked into the house after my run yesterday morning to find her at my kitchen table, drinking coffee and having banana bread with Abbey. For a minute, I thought I walked into the wrong house." I roll my eyes, feigning irritation.

But when I steal a glance across the expansive back yard as Abbey helps Dylan with my niece and nephew, I can't ignore the warmth that spreads through me. We only arrived a short while ago, yet Abbey's already charmed everyone, as if she's known these people her whole life instead of just a few minutes.

"She's a cool chic," Finn offers, his gaze trained on her as Jeremiah toddles toward her.

At a little more than a year old, he stumbles a bit on his feet, but Abbey manages to catch him before he falls. After giving him a reassuring hug, she sets him back down to continue playing.

"Good with kids, too," he adds.

"Who are we talking about?" Beckham interjects, taking a seat in the chair opposite us. "The runaway bride?"

"Who else?" Finn replies with a chuckle. "This is the most exciting thing to happen to this family since you surprised all of us by announcing your plans to marry Haley. About time you pulled your head out of your ass."

Beckham brings his glass of wine up to his lips, trying to hide his smile, but he fails miserably. His marriage to Haley may have started as a business arrangement, but there's no denying it's real now. Hell, it was real from the beginning. It just took the two of them a little longer to admit it.

"I knew there was something going on when I dropped by the taproom a few weeks ago and he was dismissive about his new employee," Beckham tells Finn, as if I'm not even here. "I found it strange he'd hire someone who didn't even know how to change a tap."

"She needed a job," I argue in my defense.

"And a place to stay?" Finn arches a brow.

"It's just temporary until she finds something else.

"Really?" He grins mischievously.

"She's my employee. And roommate. So whatever ideas you have, get them out of your head right now."

"Then you wouldn't mind if I asked her to dinner," Finn retorts with a gleam in his eye.

"Don't even fucking think about it," I growl, my response coming out harsher than I intended.

"That's what I thought." He settles back into the couch and takes another long sip of his beer.

"This is good for you," Beckham offers after a beat.

"Not you, too," I groan. "Dylan said the same thing."

"She's right. It's time you live your life again."

I part my lips, about to argue that I *have* been living my life. But what's the point? My brothers know me well enough to see through my lies.

"I know," I say with a heavy sigh, glancing toward Abbey once more, her infectious laughter like a balm to the chaos of my life.

"You're smiling." Finn nudges me.

I bring my beer bottle up to my mouth. "Shut up."

Thankfully, Mom calls us all to dinner before my brothers can tease me any further, and we all head inside. Somehow, Abbey ends up between my mom and Dylan, seamlessly blending into our family dynamic as they talk about anything that pops into their heads. Every now and then, I catch Abbey looking my way, and it sends a thrill down my spine I'm not ready to deal with.

"So, Dylan, what happened to that guy you were seeing?" Finn asks around a mouthful of lasagna, one of my mother's specialties. "The one you met at the gym?"

"We went out once. That's all." Her response is dismissive as she stabs a piece of lettuce with her fork.

"No second date?" Beckham jumps in, grinning slyly. "Is it because that's all it took for you to realize his muscles were bigger than his brain?"

"Ass." She chucks a dinner roll at him, but he reacts quickly and catches it.

"Did he speak in full sentences or just in grunts?" I chime in. "Or worse, in motivational sayings?"

"I can only imagine how things would be in the bedroom," Finn says softly so the kids can't overhear.

Thankfully, they seem to be in their own little world. Maggie, Beckham's stepdaughter, is talking animatedly about something that happened during preschool. Even though Presley doesn't talk, she still responds with facial expressions and body language. And Maggie is somehow able to figure out what she's saying.

"'No excuses. Do the work,'" Finn jokes in a strained voice, making a face to mimic lifting weights.

Or suffering from severe constipation.

"'When you feel like quitting, think about why you started,'" Beckham grunts, struggling to reel in his laughter.

"'If it doesn't challenge you, it doesn't change you,'" I offer, stealing a glimpse at Abbey, who seems to be observing our banter with interest.

"'If it's easy, you're doing it wrong,'" Hayden, the oldest of us, pipes up, unexpectedly joining in on the fun.

I smile at my brother's rare moment of humor. Lately, he's been distant, even during these monthly family dinners our mom hosts. I can't blame him. He just lost his wife.

But it's nice to hear him joke again, even if it's fleeting.

Those fleeting moments can be a big step.

They were for me all those years ago.

They still are.

"It's official. I hate all of you," Dylan says with an exaggerated roll of her eyes.

I chuckle, sipping on my beer. "We're just looking out for you, Dyl. We've got high standards for the guys who want to date our baby sister."

"You mean *impossible* standards," she fires back.

"Speaking of siblings…" Finn's voice cuts through, "do you have any brothers or sisters, Abbey?"

It's an innocent question, one most people wouldn't think twice about.

But her family is obviously a touchy subject for her.

I attempt to interject and change the topic, but Abbey answers before I have a chance.

"A few half-siblings, with another one on the way."

"That's lovely," my mom says as she takes a sip of wine. "Do you see them often?"

"I haven't seen the oldest one since I was eighteen. And I've never met the twins."

"Oh." Mom straightens in her seat, picking up on the tension in Abbey's voice.

"Abbey, it's okay if you—" I begin, but she cuts me off.

"I don't have a great relationship with my dad. I didn't even know him until I was fifteen, which is when my mom dropped me off and said I was his problem now. So while I technically have siblings, I don't have anything remotely close to all of this." She gestures around the table with a wistful look. "You're very lucky."

We all exchange glances. We may get on each other's nerves. May argue. May want to throttle each other. But hearing about Abbey's rocky family dynamic puts things into perspective.

"If you ask me, it's their loss," Mom says softly, placing a hand on top of Abbey's. "You're always welcome here, sweetie. Consider yourself an honorary Lawrence."

Abbey's mouth pinches into a tight line, like she's trying to hold back her emotions. My gaze lingers on her, noticing the slight shimmer in her eyes and the way her body seems to relax in the comforting atmosphere of our family home.

As if this is precisely where she belongs.

---

"Stop by for a chat anytime," Mom tells Abbey as she walks us to the front door after dinner. She wraps her in a tight hug, the two of them embracing in a way that makes me think they've known each other for years. Not mere days.

Even Hayden's warmed up to her, which isn't easy to pull off.

"And you better stop by the salon to see me. I'd love to get my hands on this gorgeous hair of yours." She pulls back, lifting one of Abbey's curls.

"I definitely will," she responds with a smile. "Thanks again for having me, Danielle."

"Of course." She gives Abbey one last squeeze, then turns my way.

"Dinner was delicious, Mom." I lean down and kiss her cheek. "Thanks for everything."

"Anytime." She wraps me in her embrace, then whispers, "I like her."

I want to tell her it's not like that between us, but it's not worth it. My mom won't listen anyway.

"I'll see you later on."

After I say goodbye to the rest of my siblings, as well as my niece, nephew, and Beckham's stepdaughter, I turn toward Abbey. "Ready?"

"Sure."

The car is quiet as I drive the short distance toward the historic downtown area, the hum of the engine the only noise between us. Now that we're alone, I can't stop thinking about our dinner conversation.

"What you said…," I begin cautiously, "about your mom leaving you with your father." I chance a look her way, trying to gauge her reaction. "I didn't realize it was like that."

She blows out an anxious laugh. "In retrospect, tonight probably wasn't the best time to bring it up."

"You don't have to apologize," I say dismissively. "If you haven't figured it out by now, my family is extremely laid back."

"They're some of the best people I've ever met. Which is pretty pathetic, considering I just met most of them tonight. But still. They're all great, Jude. Like really fucking incredible. I guess I just wanted to make sure you realize how lucky you are to have each other. Not many people have that."

"I know. I may fantasize about strangling my

brothers on occasion, but they're the first people I call when I need help. Mom and Dylan, too."

She gives me a small smile, then settles back into her seat, allowing another silence to fall between us as I drive along the mostly empty streets.

"My mom was really young when she had me," she announces when I pull into the driveway of my townhouse and turn off the engine. "Only fifteen, so she always saw me as a mistake. I always felt like I was more of a burden than anything else. She loved to remind me of everything she missed out on because she was raising me."

I form my hands into fists, my jaw ticking, hating she had to go through that. "That's not on you."

She nods, though I sense she doesn't truly believe it. I wonder how long she's been blaming herself for her parents' actions. Probably her entire life.

"It got worse when she met this guy. He…" She pauses, fidgeting with her hands.

"He what?" I grind out, my muscles becoming even more tense. "Did he…hurt you?"

"Not like that. It never got that far."

"That *far*?" I shoot back incredulously, ready to demand she give me his address so I can hunt him down and give him a piece of my mind.

"He made me uncomfortable."

"Did you go to your mom?"

"She didn't want to hear it. Accused me of trying to ruin her life yet again. So instead of sending him away, she packed my bags and dropped me off at my dad's. I haven't heard from her since."

A heavy silence hangs between us, the kind that feels like it could break something if I push too hard. I keep my eyes focused ahead, trying to process everything she just told me. Based on the few things she's already shared, I sensed she'd been through some stuff, but this? This is a whole other level.

It makes me see her in a way I hadn't before.

"You deserve better than that," I say quietly, finally managing to get the words out.

Abbey's piercing stare softens as she looks at me, an invisible tether pulling me closer to her, like a moth to a flame.

My heart rate picks up as my eyes trace over her plump pink lips. They look so soft and perfect, enticingly close. What would it feel like to have them move against mine? To taste her sweetness? To hear her whimper my name?

I've imagined it more times than I care to admit, the idea of losing control with her consuming me more and more each day.

Maybe this is what I need so I can finally get her out of my system. Then I can go on without constantly being haunted by her.

But I have a feeling there's no getting Abbey Rhodes out of my system. She's the worst kind of danger, the kind that seeps into your heart and soul until you no longer remember what life was like before her.

"Want to go do something?" I blurt out, pulling away before I cross the line I swore I wouldn't.

She blinks, obviously confused by the wide swing of my emotions.

So am I.

"Do something?" She furrows her brow.

"Why not? It's still early."

Plus, I sense Abbey could use a distraction right now.

Or maybe *I* could use a distraction and, for reasons I don't quite understand, I want to spend more time with her, just the two of us.

"Is there anywhere open this late on a Sunday?"

"A few places." I crank the ignition once more.

"What did you have in mind?"

I put my truck in reverse and back out of the driveway. "You'll see."

# SIXTEEN

## *Abbey*

Jude pulls into a seemingly forgotten parking lot, the faded lines and cracks in the pavement marking its age and neglect. I stare in disbelief and confusion at the neon OPEN sign flickering over the door of a rundown concrete building.

When he asked me if I wanted to do something, this was not what I had in mind. I figured we'd grab a drink at one of the bars around town. Maybe even go hang out in the brewhouse. But here we are, about to walk into a bowling alley straight out of *The Big Lebowski*.

"We're going bowling?" I remark, my voice laced with surprise.

"What's wrong with that?"

"Nothing, I just..." I shake my head. "I didn't take you for a bowler."

"I'm full of surprises," he says with a sly wink before unbuckling his seatbelt and stepping out of the truck.

"I guess so," I murmur as I follow suit.

My surprise only grows when he grabs a bag from the back of his truck — one that looks alarmingly like it holds a bowling ball.

"Is that what I think it is?" I lean closer to him and drop my voice. "Do you have your own bowling ball?"

"And if I do?" He arches a brow in challenge.

"Then this night just got even more interesting."

He places his hand on my lower back and leads me inside, my mind still trying to process the idea of serious and mercurial Jude being a regular bowler with his own custom ball.

As we step through the doors, a wave of nostalgia hits me — the smell of fried food, the faint sound of pins crashing in the distance, and the blinking lights of an ancient arcade. There was once a time I had a relatively normal childhood. A *happy* childhood. Until my grandmother died, leaving my mother to raise me. After that, nothing in my life was happy.

"Jude," a balding man greets with a small nod as we approach a counter where rows and rows of bowling shoes are neatly arranged in cubbies. "Want your usual lane?"

"If it's available."

"Sure is."

"Can I get a pair of shoes for Abbey?"

"Of course." He shifts his attention to me. "What size?"

"Eight, please."

He retrieves a pair from one of the cubbies and places them on the counter.

"Thanks, Mike," Jude says as I grab them, then steers me farther inside. It doesn't escape my notice that he didn't ask for a pair of shoes for himself, making me think he has his own.

"Usual lane?" I question.

"I just like being out of the way when I bowl."

As he leads me down the row of lanes, I scan my surroundings, taking it all in, this place that appears to be somewhere Jude frequents.

And that's when I see it. A large framed photo hangs on the wall over the bar, depicting a group of men dressed in the same shirt, a trophy displayed prominently in front of them.

In the middle stands Jude, tall and proud.

It's not even a younger version of him, either. By the looks of it, this is recent, a suspicion I confirm when I notice the year on the trophy.

I freeze, staring at the picture like I've just discovered a new species.

"Oh. My. God. You're on a bowling team?"

"League champs two years running." He

continues walking, as if it's common knowledge, but I'm too stunned by this revelation to move.

One thing is certain. Jude definitely has layers.

And I want to peel back every single one of them.

"Are you coming?" he calls after me.

I snap out of my shock and scramble to catch up.

When we reach the last lane, we both sit down. As I expected, Jude pulls a pair of his own bowling shoes out of his bag, sliding them on before standing.

"Want a beer?" he asks.

"Sure."

With a nod, he makes his way toward the bar.

There are a few other people bowling — a couple of teenagers and some older men — but at almost nine o'clock on a Sunday night, this place isn't exactly a hotbed of activity.

"Hope this is okay." Jude says when he returns holding two bottles — his label, of course.

"I'm not sure I'll ever want to drink another brand of beer again," I answer as he hands me one.

"That's what I like to hear."

I take a sip, savoring in the cold comfort of his signature IPA as it slides down my throat. Then he pulls his ball out of his bag and places it on the ball return.

"You can go first," he tells me.

"Umm… I'm terrible at this. I haven't bowled in ages. In fact, I'm pretty sure the last time I did, I was young enough to require bumpers."

"I'm sure you're not that bad. Just give it a try. I'll help if you need it."

"Don't say I didn't warn you." I pull myself to my feet and approach the ball return, testing the weight of a few of them before settling on a sparkly pink one.

Jude raises an amused brow at my choice. "I have a feeling that's meant for kids."

"It's pretty," I say in my defense. "If I'm going to make a fool out of myself, I may as well look good doing it."

"You don't need the ball for that," he replies softly, his eyes lingering on me for a moment before he clears his throat, averting his gaze. "Do you need help?"

"I'll be fine," I insist stubbornly.

I somehow manage to figure out where to put my fingers in the ball, trying to remember what I'm supposed to do from the last time I did this.

Which was easily over twenty years ago.

But it all comes back and I wind up before releasing the ball.

And just like the last time I bowled, the ball lands on the lane with a thud, bouncing a few times before ending up in the gutter.

There was definitely nothing smooth or practiced about it.

When I face Jude, his expression is a combination of shock and amusement, like he can't believe someone could be this bad at bowling. I warned him.

"Let me give you a few tips." After a quick sip of his beer, he walks toward me.

When the pink ball shoots back up into the ball return, I reach for it, but Jude stops me before I can pick it up.

"Starting with a better ball."

I playfully frown. "But it's pretty."

"And it only weighs six pounds. General rule of thumb is to use a ball that's the equivalent of ten percent of your weight, up to sixteen pounds. But beginners tend to benefit from using one that's a pound or two lighter."

"All the more reason to let me use the pink ball."

He gives me a stern look, and damn if it doesn't do things to my insides, my pulse increasing and the hairs on the back of my nape standing on end.

"Let's try a twelve-pound ball, since it's made for adults."

He scans the balls in the return before heading over to a nearby rack. After a brief perusal, he returns with a purple ball.

"Sorry it's not pink, but hopefully this will do. Give it a try and see how the weight feels."

I take it from him and insert my fingers into the three holes. "Wow. My fingers actually fit."

"Because this one isn't intended for children." He chuckles, and it sends my girly bits all aflutter. How can something as simple as a laugh make my body react like this?

But Jude's laugh isn't a regular laugh. As I've gotten to know him over the past few weeks, I've realized it's not a normal occurrence, so when he does, it's meaningful.

And it makes me want to hear him laugh more often.

"Now what?" I ask.

"Now you bowl. Let's work on your stance." He leads me toward the lane, the sound of rolling balls and clanging pins echoing around us.

"You can't stay fully upright as you release the ball, which is what you did before. And it's why your ball bounced. When you reel back, you need to bend down so the ball practically rolls out of your hand and onto the lane. Can I?" He arches a brow, his eyes raking down my frame.

"Sure," I respond, nerves dancing in my stomach.

He stands behind me, placing his hands on my hips, sending a jolt of electricity through me. I try to push away any distracting thoughts, but it's impossible when images of Jude bending me over his desk at work while he thrusts into me flood my mind.

Which is the last thing I need right now.

He keeps one hand on my left hip, extending his other arm along mine, placing his right hand beneath mine on the ball.

"Relax," he soothes, his voice low and husky, hitting me in my core.

I draw in a breath, trying to follow his command,

but I can't relax when he's this close, my breathing ragged, muscles tense.

"We're just going to practice the motion right now, so don't let go of the ball yet. Okay?"

"Okay," I answer, my voice coming out at a slightly higher pitch than I expected.

"Start with the ball in front of you," he begins, arranging me the way he wants. "Then as you pull back…" He moves my body, bringing my arm down and behind me, "you'll step forward with your right foot." He nudges my right hip with his and I step forward. "As you come forward with the ball, you'll step with your left foot, bending low at the same time."

He guides me through the motions, his body mirroring mine from behind.

"Lower," he instructs when I try to remain somewhat upright.

In my defense, it's practically impossible to concentrate when he's standing so close, his body brushing up against mine in a way that makes me want to yank him into me so I can feel every hard ripple and defined edge.

"Like this?" I ask breathily, lunging slightly.

"Yeah." I can hear the subtle tremble in his voice. "Like that."

His head dips closer to my neck, his breath hot on my skin. I take a deep inhale, my body wound tighter than it has been in recent memory. Maybe ever.

Despite the somewhat uncomfortable position, I don't move. Don't want him to stop touching me. Don't want him to stop breathing me in. Don't want to stop feeling his lips so close, a fire igniting deep inside.

After what feels like too short of a time, he guides me back to standing and increases the space between us.

"Go ahead and try it on your own now."

I take a moment to push down my disappointment from the lack of contact.

"Oh, and one more thing."

"Yeah?" I snap my eyes toward his.

"Don't aim for the center pin."

"What do you mean?"

"Most beginners aim for that center pin. You want to aim for the space between the center pin and the one behind it to the right, since you're right handed. Trust me."

"Okay." I turn from him, standing straight with my eyes focused on the spot he mentioned.

With a deep breath, I go through the motions he taught me, the ball rolling out of my hand and onto the lane without the usual thump and bounce.

My heart races as I watch the ball travel closer and closer to the pins. It grazes the bumper, but doesn't fall in, knocking down a single pin on the side.

Unable to contain my enthusiasm, I jump up and down, clapping like I just hit a strike instead of one measly pin.

"Good job," Jude praises with a smile, those damn dimples popping again. "Keep practicing and you'll be hitting strikes in no time."

As we continue to bowl over the next few hours, I get a little better. Or maybe it's the beer loosening me up and making me *think* I'm getting better.

Whenever it's my turn, Jude helps adjust my form or offers me a tip.

And whenever it's his turn, I can't help but admire his easy confidence. Not to mention, his ass looks incredible in his jeans as he bends down, the muscles in his arms flexing and rippling.

I never thought bowling could turn me on. That was before I watched Jude Lawrence bowl. Pretty sure this man could make even the most mundane tasks look sexy.

"How did you get into bowling?" I ask after he hits yet another strike.

Show off.

"My dad." He tips back his bottle, slowly nursing his beer since he's driving. "He didn't start bowling until after he was diagnosed with ALS. He'd take us kids on occasion, but wasn't serious about it until he learned he'd never be able to do it again. After his diagnosis, he had a bucket list of everything he wanted to do."

"What kind of things were on it?" I ask, wanting to know more about this man who's obviously been a huge influence on Jude's life.

"There were all the usual things. Go to Paris. Float in the Dead Sea. See the Aurora Borealis. But he also had some more personal items."

I lean toward him. "Like what?"

"Like making my mom laugh every day. Letting all of us kids know how much he loved us. Learning to let go of the small stuff," he says with a wistful smile. "He believed that not every meaningful experience should require a flight or advanced planning. Some bucket list items should be checked off every day."

A pang of sadness tugs at my heart as I consider the bittersweet memories Jude must have of his father. With each story he shares, I learn more and more about Jude. Peel back more and more of his layers.

"I wish I could have met him," I admit softly.

"He definitely would have liked you."

A comfortable silence settles between us as we stare at each other for several long moments. Then I clear my throat and stand. "Guess it's my turn."

"Yeah."

I grab my ball and walk toward our lane, lining myself up.

Without a single tip or correction from Jude, I end up knocking down more pins than I ever have, leaving only three standing.

"Not trying to make you nervous or anything," Jude says as the automatic system clears the fallen pins, returning the others to their place, "but you have a pretty good opportunity for a spare."

I glance to the end of the lane, noting the pins left are all in a cluster on the left side.

"You see those arrows on the lane?" He approaches, pointing to a series of brown markings painted on the wood.

I nod.

"Try to send the ball down the second one from the left. Okay?"

"Got it."

"Good." He squeezes my arm.

I turn back toward the lane, focusing on the spot Jude instructed. I shouldn't be this nervous. It's not like this game matters. But I want to impress Jude.

And I want to prove to myself I can do this.

I briefly close my eyes, practicing some of my breathing techniques from yoga. When I open them again, I pull the ball back and it slides easily off my fingers, heading down the lane.

Right down the second arrow.

I straighten, holding my breath as the ball turns over. And over. And over.

When it hits the pins, the clatter echoes around me, every pin falling...

Except one.

But the one remaining wobbles.

Left. Right. Left.

I don't breathe. Don't think. Just watch that damn pin, begging it to fall.

When it finally does, I shriek, "I did it!"

Without thinking, I run toward Jude and throw my arms around him. His hand goes to my back, and he pulls me against him, his touch sending ripples through me. When I feel his breath against my neck, my laughter instantly dies, my pulse increasing.

"Great job, Abbey," he murmurs.

I pull back slightly and meet his eyes. The warmth in them makes my heart do a stupid little flip. His gaze dips to my lips, like it did in his truck earlier tonight. For a second, I think he's going to kiss me. I *want* him to. Want him to close that tiny gap between us. Want him to forget about everything holding him back and just do it.

But like in the truck earlier, the realization of what he's about to do hits and he releases me, taking a step back.

Even with space between us, the tension in the air is still charged. Electric. On the brink of combusting.

"Guess you're not so bad at bowling after all," he says, rubbing the back of his neck.

I swallow down the renewed wave of disappointment. "I had a good coach."

# SEVENTEEN

## *Abbey*

The crisp scent of citrus surrounds me as I carefully return the contents to their rightful place in the freshly cleaned refrigerator. My hands are slightly rough and my arms ache from scrubbing every inch of this townhouse from top to bottom.

With all the hours I've worked at the taproom and the generous tips I've received from many locals, I've been able to save a decent amount of money.

More money than I made in a month at my nonprofit job.

Despite being in a good position to pay rent, Jude still refuses to accept a single penny from me. Instead, I've made sure to contribute in other ways, like buying groceries and other household necessities.

But a couple hundred bucks on groceries seems

inadequate compared to everything he's done for me, so I decided to use my day off today to clean the townhouse. It's not a disaster zone by any means — Jude's a pretty tidy roommate — but it's probably been a while since anyone's given the floors and countertops a good scrub.

When I lived with Carson, I hated spending an entire day cleaning. With him, cleaning and cooking were expected duties, since he was supporting me financially, even if he was the one to suggest it.

It's different with Jude. He's never once asked anything of me, other than being on time for work and friendly to his customers. Which is why I don't mind spending my day cleaning. I *want* to do something nice for him in return for all the kindness he's shown me.

I sing along with Chappell Roan on one of my playlists, not caring who might see or hear. I shouldn't be this happy while cleaning. But since arriving in Sycamore Falls and being welcomed like I've always lived here, it's difficult *not* to be happy.

To not feel like I belong.

During my time here, I've formed amazing friendships I'll remember for the rest of my life.

Every Monday morning, I have a standing coffee date with Jude's mother, where she catches me up on the latest gossip she's picked up while working at the salon.

Every other Wednesday, I attend a meeting of the

unofficial Sycamore Falls Dirty Book Club, which Dylan convinced me to join, along with Haley, Beckham's wife, their friend, Parker, and the beloved Grandma Estelle. Even though she's not technically a grandmother, I can see why everyone in town loves and admires her. She's a riot to be around, and is responsible for my discovery of a genre of romance I didn't think was needed — monster erotica.

But my favorite thing to do is go bowling with Jude on Sunday night. It's become the highlight of my week.

I'd like to think it's become the highlight of Jude's week, too.

Over the past several weeks, I've definitely improved. I'm not nearly as good as Jude, but a spare isn't a rarity anymore. In fact, I've even managed to hit a few strikes.

I've only been here for a little over a month, but I can't imagine being anywhere else at this point in my life. While I know I can't stay here forever, this place is what I need right now. It's helped heal my soul and give me hope. Maybe that's why I haven't actively started to look for a job in my field yet. Because once I find one, I'll have to say goodbye to Sycamore Falls. I'm not ready to do that quite yet.

With the refrigerator cleaner and more organized than it's probably been in ages, I set my sights on mopping the floors.

Provided Jude owns some sort of mop.

I check in all the obvious places — the entryway closet, laundry room, garage — but come up empty. Maybe he doesn't have one.

I'm about to walk down to the hardware store to grab one when I remember the closed door on the second floor. It must be a closet. Maybe it's in there.

Heading up the stairs, I walk past my bedroom and approach the door opposite the guest bathroom. As I do, an unsettling chill trickles down my spine, a strange premonition washing over me.

What if I'm wrong? What if it's not a closet, but a room he's kept closed for some reason? But what would that be?

Because he's a modern-day Norman Bates and is keeping a mummified version of his mother in this room? That's ridiculous. Not to mention, I'm more than aware his mother is alive and well.

And not a mummy.

Shaking off my unease, I place my hand on the doorknob and turn. As the door opens with a loud creak, every inch of me freezes in place.

I was wrong.

This isn't a closet.

It's a room.

And not just any room.

It's a nursery.

The blinds are drawn tight, allowing only a few slivers of light to filter through. The air feels heavy and stagnant, a thick layer of dust coating every surface, confirming my suspicion that no one has entered this room in quite some time.

I should turn around and walk away. Pretend I never saw it.

If I thought snooping through Jude's room and finding that ultrasound photo was an invasion of his privacy, this is even worse. Then again, I *do* live here. Did he expect I wouldn't eventually find this room? It's a miracle I haven't stumbled on it until now.

That's all the rationale I need to propel me forward into the darkened space.

A photo of Jude and a beautiful brunette sits on a white dresser, her pregnant belly proudly on display. The pale pink wall behind the crib is adorned with a mural of sleeping baby animals, a matching mobile hanging overhead.

Everything's frozen in time, waiting for a baby that never came.

The thought makes my heart squeeze, my throat closing up.

No wonder he was so cynical the night we met. If I'd suffered this kind of loss, I'd be angry at the world, too. It's obvious this child was wanted — desperately so. I can picture Jude constructing the furniture, painting the walls, whispering his hopes and dreams for the baby against her mother's belly.

And now all those hopes and dreams are gone.

What happened?

I'm not sure I want to know.

Regardless, one thing is certain — Jude's past holds secrets and a pain I'll never truly comprehend or imagine. And now, standing in this deserted nursery, I can't help but feel even more sorrow and sympathy for him.

"*What the fuck are you doing?!*"

A harsh voice startles me, and I whirl around, inhaling sharply. Jude looms just on the other side of the doorway, his presence filling the room even though he doesn't step inside. His face is contorted in anger, his dark eyes boring into mine.

I try to speak, but my words are caught in my throat from the intensity of his fury. His body is taut, jaw clenched, muscles straining.

"*Answer me!*"

"I… I was just looking for a mop," I stammer out. "I've been cleaning the house today and thought—"

"*Get out!*" he snaps, his voice sharp enough to cut me in half.

Without hesitation, I scurry from the room as quickly as possible.

"You're never to step foot in this room," he admonishes, his gaze fixed on me like I've committed some kind of crime.

Then again, I have.

"*Ever.* Do you understand?"

"I'm sorry. I didn't know it was…" I trail off, unsure how to finish that statement. A nursery? A child's room?

A reminder of what could have been?

"I don't care what you did or didn't know," he interrupts coldly. "I keep this door closed for a reason." He slams it shut, the harsh sound causing me to jump. "Don't ever go in there again."

The intensity in his eyes leaves no room for argument.

"I'm sorry," I offer, lowering my head and hurrying down the stairs, my entire body surging with adrenaline.

As soon as I enter the kitchen, I place my hands on the counter and take several deep breaths, trying to calm myself. But even down here, the weight of Jude's anger hangs heavy in the air.

"You should find somewhere else to live," his voice pierces the silence.

Instead of the pure rage I heard mere seconds ago, his words are soft, but they still cut just as deep.

I face him, searching his cold, unforgiving stare. "What do you mean?" I blink, my throat tight.

"I told you from the beginning this wasn't permanent. I'm not so sure having a roommate is a good idea for me."

"But—"

"I'm not going to throw you out onto the street. Just...try to find somewhere else. I'll even help pay for it."

"You'll pay my rent so I don't have to live here?"

He hesitates, as if reconsidering. Then he shakes his head. "I can't have you here anymore."

The finality in his statement stings more than it should, wrapping around me like a weighted chain.

Then he turns, his footfalls heavy as he walks out of the house. When the door slams closed behind him, I release a shaky breath, feeling like I've been kicked out of a place I was just beginning to think of as home.

But even as I wipe away the tears that have escaped, I can't stop thinking about the nursery, the baby that was supposed to be...and the man who's still tormented by her absence.

# EIGHTEEN

## *Abbey*

"Are you going to tell me what happened between you and my brother?" Dylan asks as I pour a few lagers for a handful of golfers. "Or do I have to get you drunk to finally get you to come clean?"

"What are you talking about?" I ask dismissively, purposefully avoiding so much as stealing a glance in the direction of the brewhouse.

It's been almost two weeks since the nursery incident, and I've spent every minute of them doing my best to avoid Jude.

Truthfully, it hasn't been difficult.

He's been just as eager to avoid me, spending his days locked away in the brewhouse and not coming home until long after I've already gone to bed. Hell, some days I'm not sure if he's even come home. In fact, I'm certain he hasn't, since I've shown up to work more than once, only to find him wearing the same clothes he wore the previous day.

I don't know what hurts more — him telling me to find somewhere else to live or the fact that I feel like an intruder all over again. Like I don't belong.

"I'm not stupid." Dylan narrows her gaze on me. "Or blind. Up until last week, my brother was smiling. He was happy."

I part my lips to argue, but she cuts me off.

"And I know it's because of you," she continues, her voice dropping.

"We're not. We haven't—"

"I'm not saying you were sleeping together or anything, but he's definitely been more tolerable. At least he was. Now he's back to the way he used to be. Since all I've been able to get out of him are a few grunts mixed in with the occasional 'fuck off', I've decided to come to you instead." Her expression softens with genuine concern. "What's going on, Abbey?"

I stare at her for several long moments and chew on my bottom lip, unsure what to tell her.

Will she be just as upset about my actions as Jude was?

She's the closest thing I have to a friend, and the idea of losing her because of this guts me. It's one of the reasons I told Danielle I couldn't get together for coffee this week.

But I don't know how much longer I can carry this weight. I need to tell someone.

I look around to make sure none of the other servers are eavesdropping, then admit, "I found the nursery."

My confession hangs in the air, echoing around me, drowning out the music playing in the background.

She straightens, her eyes wide and mouth agape. Based on her response, she knows exactly what room I'm talking about.

"You… How?"

I lick my lips before answering in a hushed tone, "I was cleaning and couldn't find a mop, so I went upstairs to look in what I thought was a closet. But it wasn't a closet."

"It's not," she says with a hint of remorse. For what? Not warning me?

What would she have even said?

*Hey, just so you know, don't go into the closed room on the second floor because there's an untouched nursery?*

It wasn't her job to warn me.

"Everything in there… It's like time just stopped. I know I should have left the instant I realized what it was," I add quickly in my defense. "I couldn't help it. It was so…"

"Sad?" Dylan offers in understanding.

"Heartbreaking, Dylan. It was fucking heartbreaking." I grab a dishrag and start to wipe down the bar in the hopes of distracting myself from the memory. I can only imagine how it must affect Jude.

"And let me guess… You mentioned it to him," Dylan remarks, leaning against the counter and taking a sip of her water.

I slowly shake my head and lift my eyes to hers. "He found me in it."

"Fuck…," she exhales.

"He completely lost it, Dylan. I've never seen anyone so angry before. And then…"

"Yes?" She leans closer.

"He told me it was best if I found somewhere else to live. So that's what I've been doing when I'm not here. Sitting in the library and using one of the computers there to search for a job and a short-term rental. There are a lot of vacation rentals around, but they're all booked solid. I was able to get on a few waitlists. I guess a part of me is hoping to hear back about a job. It doesn't make sense to go through the hassle of finding somewhere to live if I'm not staying. I've thought about taking what money I've saved and just...leaving. Maybe go to Reno while I figure out what's next."

"Do you *want* to leave?" She arches a brow.

That's the million dollar question. One I haven't been able to wrap my head around. Leaving is probably the smart thing to do. What makes the most sense. After all, I was only supposed to stay until I got back on my feet. Since I haven't had to pay any rent or other bills, I've been able to save quite a bit of money.

But the idea of leaving this place and never seeing any of these people again makes my stomach knot.

"I… I don't know," I admit as I stare into space.

"Listen, Abbey…" Dylan steps toward me. "As much as I'd like to tell you the story behind that nursery and why seeing you in there set Jude off, it's not mine to tell. It's Jude's. And Krista's."

"His ex?" I ask cautiously.

She nods solemnly.

"I saw her photo in the nursery. She's very pretty."

"You actually remind me of her."

"I do?" I ask, unsure how to feel about that. Did Jude only show me the kindness he did because I remind him of his ex?

"She was incredibly optimistic, just like you. It didn't matter how bad things got, she always looked on the bright side. But Jude…" She trails off. "He's been through so much. That nursery? It's part of it."

"I was just starting to feel like I had a home here and now…" I trail off.

"You *do* have a home here." She grabs my hand and gives it a squeeze. "Jude's just… He's carrying a lot. Sometimes he doesn't know how to handle it."

"I get it. I do. Especially after seeing that nursery.

But I don't like feeling unwelcome, which is exactly how he's made me feel."

"Don't give up just yet, okay?" She gives me an encouraging look. "He'll come around. I know it. You just have to be patient. Plus, I really don't want you to go."

"Why? Because then you'll have to work more hours at the taproom again?" I joke, trying to lighten the mood.

"No. I mean, yes. There's that." She rolls her eyes.

Once I started working here, she only had to come in to cover a handful of shifts, giving her some much needed time to herself. Lately, however, more and more people have been calling out. Probably because they don't want to deal with our moody boss.

"But that's not the only reason I want you to stay."

"It's not?"

"You're my friend." She shrugs. "And I'd rather not lose my friend because of my idiot brother."

Her words tug at something inside me. Maybe I don't have a family, but in some weird way, I've started to build one here without even realizing.

"You won't lose me," I assure her. "No matter what, we'll remain friends. Idiot brother or not."

"Good."

"On that note…" I place the beers I just poured onto a tray. "I should drop these off before they complain to the boss about slow service. He's been impossible lately."

"You're telling me," Dylan retorts.

Carefully balancing my tray, I head toward the patio and drop off the beers. After taking an order from a group of tourists who just sat down, I make my way back inside, purposefully looking anywhere other than the brewhouse.

Which is when someone stands from a nearby table, stepping in front of me.

"Excuse me." I attempt to sidestep him.

But he wraps his hand around my arm, preventing me from doing so.

"What are—"

The question on my tongue disappears as I peer into a pair of familiar blue eyes, sending my heart plummeting to the pit of my stomach.

And I thought today couldn't get any worse.

I was wrong.

# NINETEEN

## *Jude*

The low hum of the fermentation tanks fills the brewhouse, creating a comforting background noise as I make meticulous notes on my clipboard. The taproom is starting to get busy now that it's almost five on a Friday afternoon. But in here, no one bothers me. Instead, I can lose myself in my work.

But no matter how much I've tried to distract myself with work, thoughts of Abbey creep back in.

Things between us have definitely been strained lately. To avoid running into her, I've locked myself away in the brewhouse whenever she's working.

Like right now.

Although that hasn't stopped me from checking on her every so often. And every time I look her way, I see the uncertainty in her expression and feel like an asshole all over again.

But it's not enough to make me apologize.

Or explain what she saw.

The sound of the door creaking open pulls me from my thoughts. I glance up to see Finn standing in the doorway, his hands nonchalantly tucked into his pockets, as if he doesn't have a care in the world.

"Whatcha doing?" he asks, his voice casual.

"What does it look like? I'm working." I turn back to the papers in front of me, trying to make it clear I'm not in the mood for a conversation.

Finn doesn't take the hint. He never does. Instead, he continues farther into the brewhouse, hoisting himself onto the stainless steel table I'm currently sitting at.

I'm beginning to regret giving him the code to the brewhouse.

"Are you planning to tell me what's going on, or do I have to beat it out of you?"

"You'd lose."

"Maybe. Want to find out?"

"There's nothing going on," I snap, staring at the papers in front of me, all my brewing notes blurring together.

Finn raises a skeptical brow, clearly not buying it. "Word on the street is you've made quite a few of your employees cry. Some are even threatening to quit."

"I haven't been that bad," I attempt to argue in my defense, but my voice lacks any sort of conviction.

I *have* been an ass. But it's easier than trying to make sense of my conflicting feelings about Abbey. One minute, I want to push her away and forget I ever met her, scared of the things she makes me feel. The next, I want to wrap her in my arms and beg for forgiveness.

"The entire town has been placing bets on whether you'll kill or fuck each other first," Finn remarks.

"What are you talking about?"

"You and Abbey. Of course, my money is on you two attempting to kill each other but ending up fucking instead. Unless you already have."

"Why can't people in this town mind their own goddamn business?" I roll my eyes. "Abbey and me… We're fine."

"Fine?" he retorts. "Nothing about you has been fine for over a week. You're treating everyone like shit. Which makes me think something happened between you and Abbey."

"It's not what you think," I sigh, leaning back in my chair and running a hand over my face.

"What is it then? Because the tension between you two is hard to miss. Hell, I feel it right now, and she's out in the fucking taproom." He waves his hand toward the windows, and I glance up just as she passes carrying a tray of beer.

Despite everything, a subtle fluttering erupts in my stomach at the sight of her. I hate that I have no control over my reaction to her. And maybe that's what this is all about. That I'm actually feeling things again, and I have no idea what to do about it.

"I found her in the nursery last week," I admit softly.

Finn's expression drops, his eyes wide with concern. "Shit."

"I completely lost it," I continue, the tightness in my chest growing. "Screamed at her to get out. Told her to find somewhere else to live."

"Did she know you didn't want her to go in there?"

"I thought about mentioning something, but I didn't want to raise her suspicions."

"So she didn't know it was off limits?"

"Well…no, but—"

"You need to get rid of that room," Finn declares, cutting me off. "It's not healthy. Staying in that town-house probably isn't healthy, either, if I'm being honest. You're trapped by all the memories and it's fucking killing you."

"I'm fine," I try to insist.

"No, you're not, you stubborn ass. You're anything but fine. What do you hope to accomplish by staying in that house? By keeping that nursery intact? You can't keep living like this. You can't keep torturing yourself like this. It's holding you back from…" He trails off.

"From what, Finn? What's it holding me back from?" I snarl, getting into his face. But he doesn't back down.

He never does.

"From moving on. And I think that's what you're really upset about. You don't care that Abbey was in the nursery. You're upset that she saw a side you've been trying to hide from everyone. This isn't about a nursery, Jude. It's about *you*."

I vehemently shake my head, on the brink of telling him he doesn't know what he's talking about when something in the taproom catches my attention.

Abbey's talking to a guy in a suit, which normally wouldn't cause the hair on my nape to stand on end. But there's something about him that has me on edge. I don't like the way he's looking at her. Don't like her defensive stance.

When she attempts to retreat and he grabs her, every rational thought I possess goes out the window.

Pushing past my brother, I storm out of the brewhouse, my sole focus on one thing and one thing only. Getting to Abbey.

# TWENTY

## *Abbey*

"Carson?" My voice is barely above a whisper as I stare into his eyes in complete shock.

How is he here?

Am I imagining this?

It can't be real.

But when his grip on my arm tightens, I know it *is* real.

"Surprised to see me?" He smirks, his tone laced with amusement as he releases his hold on me, adjusting the tie of his designer suit, not a single thread out of place.

"What are you doing here?" I take a small step back.

"I'm in Tahoe for a meeting and thought I'd use the opportunity to pick up the car you stole."

I open my mouth to remind him it was a gift, but he cuts me off.

Much like he often did during our relationship.

"I've heard good things about this beer, so I decided to stop in. Imagine my surprise when I saw you working here. What are the chances?" Based on the conniving grin curling on his lips, he knew full well I've been working here.

"I need to get back to work." I attempt to push past him, but he blocks my path.

"Hasn't this gone on long enough?"

"What are you talking about?"

"This little temper tantrum. I get it. You're pissed. You want me to grovel? Fine." He places his hands together, pretending to be remorseful. "I made a mistake and it won't happen again. Please forgive me." His words come out rushed and devoid of any regret.

"Forgive you?" I throw my head back and laugh. "You fucked my best friend, Carson. Ten minutes before we were supposed to get married. When I broke things off, you canceled all my cards and reported the car you gave me as stolen."

"Stop being so dramatic. I apologized, so let's move on and try again."

"Try again?" I repeat.

He's more delusional than I thought.

Or narcissistic.

"You should be happy I ran out on you. Now

you're free to stick your dick in anyone you want without ramifications."

"It's not that easy," he says through gritted teeth.

"Sure it is," I say nonchalantly. "Insert peg A into slot B. Would you like me to draw you a picture?"

"Enough with the jokes, Abbey…"

Jaw ticking, he grabs my arm, his nostrils flaring with barely contained frustration. This time his grip on me is harsh, causing me to wince.

"You royally fucked me when you ran out on our wedding. I'm losing clients, since some prefer to work with advisors with certain…values."

"Such as not having an affair with a subordinate co-worker?" I ask, attempting to pull my arm free.

But he only grips me tighter.

"You *need* me, Abbey." His words are low and threatening. "I'm all you have. I'm the only one who's ever cared, and you're acting like a spoiled brat. So if I were you——"

"You're wrong."

At the sound of the deep, gravelly voice, Carson drops his hold on me and spins around.

I snap my head to my right as Jude moves in beside me, Finn standing just off to the side, not letting Carson out of his sight.

"She's not alone." Jude's intense gaze bores into Carson with pure hatred and disgust, his presence oddly comforting, despite the past several days. "And she sure as hell doesn't need you."

Carson straightens, his smug expression faltering for a moment. "Who the hell are you?"

Jude doesn't flinch, his voice calm but laced with danger. "I'm the guy who's telling you to leave her alone. Now."

"We're having a civil conversation."

"From where I was standing, it didn't look all that civil to me. No one comes into my place of business and assaults my employees."

"I didn't—"

"Don't fucking lie to me. I know what I saw." He crosses his arms in front of his chest and widens his stance, showcasing his rather impressive muscles. Finn does the same, the two Lawrence brothers a force to be reckoned with. "I'll give you one more chance to walk out of those doors. Otherwise, you'll be escorted out of them in handcuffs for trespassing."

"I'm not trespassing. This is a public establishment. I'm still drinking my beer."

A surge of defiance rises within me, and I grab his glass off the table. Tilting it, I dump the contents over his head, watching with delight as it soaks his perfect suit.

"Beer's gone," I taunt.

He stares at me, mouth agape, his face turning red with fury. "You fucking bitch. You—"

Jude positions himself in front of me once more, his posture stiff, expression unwavering. "Last chance.

Leave. *Now.* Otherwise, a little beer on your suit will be the least of your worries."

For a moment, it feels like time freezes. The air between the men crackles with tension, and I can sense the impending fight. It wouldn't even be a contest. Jude could easily overpower Carson if he wanted to. Throw Finn into the mix and it's a no-brainer. Carson doesn't stand a chance.

Probably sensing this, he huffs, deliberately bumping into Jude as he storms out of the taproom, his wet clothes sloshing around him.

As soon as he disappears, Jude turns to me, his eyes awash with concern. It's so different from the harsh, unforgiving stares I've grown used to lately. Now, he looks like the Jude he was before it all went to shit.

"Are you okay?" He rakes his gaze over my frame, searching for any bruising or marks.

"I…" I shake my head, struggling to find the right words. "That felt really fucking good." A laugh escapes my lips, releasing the tension that's been building inside of me.

"Good," he exhales in relief.

Without hesitation, he wraps his arms around me, pulling me against his chest. Surprised by his affectionate gesture, I stiffen, reeling from his embrace. But as I inhale his familiar scent, I melt into him, savoring in his warmth, regardless of how fleeting it most likely is.

Too soon, he drops his hold on me and steps away, as if I have some contagious disease.

As if remembering he's supposed to hate me.

"Come get me when your shift is over. I'll walk you home."

"You don't—"

He holds a hand up, cutting me off and narrowing his gaze at me. "There's no way in hell I'm letting you walk by yourself after what just happened. Don't fight me on this." He lowers his voice to a level I haven't heard in nearly two weeks. "Please."

It's impossible to deny him when he asks like this, even though all rationale tells me I should.

"Okay," I finally concede.

"Okay." A small smile teases his lips, but it vanishes just as quickly.

"See." Dylan nudges me as I watch him disappear into the brewhouse with Finn. "I told you he'd eventually come around."

I roll my eyes, pretending not to care. "Don't hold your breath."

# TWENTY-ONE

## *Jude*

A tense silence hangs heavy in the space between Abbey and me as I walk her to my townhouse after closing the taproom. With it being a Friday night, a few people are out and about, most of them heading to one of the other bars in the downtown area. Other than that, the streets are quiet.

Which only serves to amplify the unease between us.

It doesn't help that my mind keeps replaying Finn's words from earlier today. How I can't keep living like this.

I know he's right. But how the hell am I supposed to move on when everything in me feels like it's tied to the past?

I try to focus on the rhythm of my footsteps, hoping it might help me work things out in my head.

It doesn't.

With each step, the tension surrounding me feels like a noose, squeezing me tighter and tighter until I'm convinced I'll suffocate unless I finally release this pressure.

"I was married," I blurt out as Abbey is about to disappear inside my townhouse.

She stops in her tracks, but doesn't immediately look at me, several long seconds ticking by. Finally, she meets my gaze from over her shoulder, a mixture of compassion and confusion in her blue eyes.

"We met in college," I explain, my voice hoarse. "She was everything I thought I wanted. Beautiful, intelligent, ambitious. We made all these plans and I couldn't wait to build a life with her. We faced a few obstacles here and there, especially when I dropped out of school, but we made the distance work. When she graduated and took a job in Lake Tahoe, I didn't hesitate. I proposed right away."

Abbey fully faces me, her gaze softening. I don't know why I suddenly feel compelled to share all of this with her, but I can't stop the words from pouring out. With each one, it becomes a little easier to breathe.

"Everyone said we were too young — only twenty-three — but we didn't care. We were happy. And when she told me she was pregnant several years later, I was so excited about starting a family with her. Everything was perfect..." My throat tightens and I struggle to swallow back the knot forming. "Until it wasn't."

Pinching my lips together in a tight line, I fight to push down the surge of emotions bubbling up inside me as I relive the worst moment of my life. When Abbey reaches for my hand and intertwines our fingers, it gives me the strength and reassurance to continue.

"Krista went into labor early. Thirty weeks." My voice cracks, the memory clawing at me. "Our little girl fought so hard, but in the end, we lost her." I blink back the tears threatening to fall. "After that, we lost each other."

Abbey parts her lips, but I cut her off, needing to get this all out before I change my mind.

"Every time I walked into that room afterwards, it was like reliving it all over again. The hope, the excitement, the pain...it's all there. It's why I've done nothing with that space. And when I saw you in there..." I trail off, shaking my head. "I shouldn't have yelled at you. I just didn't know how to deal with it."

"I'm so sorry," she whispers, her voice trembling.

"You have nothing to apologize for. I was an ass to you, Abbey. And it wasn't because you were in the nursery."

She tilts her head, her brow creasing. "It wasn't?"

"No."

"Then—"

"You scare the shit out of me," I confess.

Surprise flickers in her eyes. "What do you mean?"

"You make me want more."

I cup her face, closing the gap between us until our breaths intermingle in the warm night air.

"You make me feel things I haven't let myself feel in a long time, and I don't know what I'm supposed to think about that."

My declaration hangs in the air between us, echoing in the stillness of the night. I half expect for her to push me away. Tell me she could never forgive me for how I've treated her these past several days. Honestly, she *shouldn't* forgive me.

But then her lips curve up into the same enigmatic smile that drew me to her when we first met, making me want to know all her secrets.

As she presses her body against mine, I can feel her warmth. Her understanding. Her forgiveness.

I don't deserve it. Don't deserve her.

But when her mouth inches closer, I don't care. The heaviness in my chest fades away, and I focus on her and her alone. Not my pain. Not my regrets. Just Abbey, and the way she makes me feel more alive than I thought possible.

"Maybe you should stop thinking," she says, husky and wanton.

"And do what?"

"Maybe you should feel instead." Her lips hover achingly close to mine. "Feel me, Jude."

Her words are like a siren's call, stirring something inside me I can't ignore. Any lingering resistance evaporates, and I slam my mouth against her, electricity shooting through my veins at the feel of her lips moving with mine. I've fantasized about kissing her more times than I care to admit. Even when I was trying to avoid her.

She tastes even better than I imagined, her tongue gliding against mine as if this is a dance we've done dozens of times before, consuming me until I can no longer breathe.

I tear away, panting in an attempt to regain some control over myself.

"We… We shouldn't do this," I manage to say.

"Oh." Her expression falls, and she averts her gaze. "Right. Bad idea since you're technically my boss and all that. Sorry." She starts to head inside.

But before she can get far, I grab a hold of her wrist and pull her back against me. Nuzzling my face into her neck, I rasp out, "I don't mean we shouldn't do this at all."

"Then wha—"

"Mrs. Whitman lives across the street and loves to report on everything she observes in the neighborhood."

I pull back and trace my gaze over her face.

Piercing blue eyes. Slender nose. Plump lips I'm lucky enough to know how they taste.

"I don't know about you, but I'd rather keep my sex life private."

She smirks, hoisting herself onto her toes. "You're being a bit presumptuous, aren't you?"

"Perhaps," I begin, placing my hand on her hip and steering her into the house, kicking the door closed behind us. "Although I prefer to think of it as setting a goal and developing a plan to achieve it. It's not a completely unrealistic one. In fact, if you ask me, it would qualify as a SMART goal."

"A SMART goal?" She raises an inquisitive brow.

"Precisely." I give her a wicked look as I press her against the wall. "Specific, measurable, achievable, realistic, and timely. Obviously, it's specific enough. I want to put my cock in your pussy and make you see stars."

Her complexion turns red, and I love that I have this effect on her. Even so, she doesn't shy away. If anything, she wants to hear more.

"And measurable?" she coos, batting her lashes. "How will you measure your progress?"

"I can just look at you to find out how close I am to achieving it."

"How so?"

"Seeing as your breathing has increased and you keep moistening your lips, I'd say those are reliable indicators of whether I'm progressing toward my goal." I curve toward her, nipping at her skin. "I'd bet if I ran my fingers along your panties right now, they'd be soaked. Am I right?"

"Maybe," she exhales before taking a moment to compose herself. "What about achievable?"

"I'd like to think it is. And then some." I wink.

"Relevant?" Her question drips with lust as she peers at me through hooded lids.

"I can't think of a more relevant goal at the moment," I answer gruffly, grinding my hips against her, letting her feel just how relevant it is.

"Timely?" she whimpers, briefly closing her eyes as she basks in the feel of me.

"God, I fucking hope so." I bury my head in her neck, desperate to lose myself in her.

"Well then…" She drapes an arm over my shoulder and rakes her fingers through my hair. "Let's see if I can help you achieve your goal."

"I was hoping you'd say that," I growl.

Then I crush my lips back against hers.

# TWENTY-TWO

## *Abbey*

I didn't think this was possible.

I'm not surprised that Jude would be kissing me. Or that we just had a conversation about how his goal tonight is to sleep with me.

Instead, I didn't think it possible that a kiss could make me feel like this. So lightheaded. So breathless. So out of control.

But in the best way imaginable.

"Hold on," he rasps.

Before I can ask what he means by that, he grips my ass, forcing my legs around his waist as he lifts me, carrying me up the stairs as if I weigh nothing.

When we reach his room, he places me onto the bed, his gaze sharp and assessing.

I haven't been back in here since the morning I

snooped. But unlike that morning, the lighting is dim, masking the fact that he once shared this bed with someone else.

With someone he loved.

Maybe someone he still does.

Jude crawls on top of me and reclaims my mouth, his harsh kiss erasing the idea from my mind. Explosive currents race through my body, becoming more intense as his erection hits that spot I'm desperate to feel him, and I release a moan.

"Just like I imagined," he croons before diving in for another kiss, hard and searching.

"What did you imagine?"

"How you'd sound." He trails kisses from my lips and down my neck, his teeth nipping slightly. "But that's not all I thought about."

"It's not?"

I meet his dark gaze and he slowly shakes his head, the look in his eyes causing my pulse to race.

"What else did you think about?"

"These tits."

He cups them through my shirt, squeezing my sensitive nipples. A sharp gasp escapes my lips as pleasure and pain blend together, an inferno burning me from the inside out.

"How they'd feel," he continues. "How you'd react when I took your nipple between my teeth."

"Then why don't you find out?" I exhale.

"Gladly." Reaching for the hem of my shirt, he arches a single brow.

We can stop this right now, refuse to cross the line that's been murky between us from the beginning. A voice in my head tells me that's exactly what I should do. That Jude's the kind of man who will completely eviscerate my heart.

But I don't care about that. Not when I'm desperate to feel him.

With a nod, I sit up and allow him to take off my shirt. Once he lifts it over my head, I unhook my bra, tossing it onto the floor.

"Goddamn." His pupils dilate with hunger as he lowers me back against the mattress, taking my breasts in his hands.

I close my eyes and savor in his touch, especially when he lowers his mouth to one nipple, circling his tongue around it before taking it between his teeth. When he nibbles, I can't help but moan, my core clenching, body throbbing with want.

"What else?" I pant, struggling to catch my breath.

He meets my gaze. "What's that?"

"What else did you imagine?"

A sly grin tugs on his mouth and he returns his lips to my breasts before snaking down my body, exploring every inch like I'm an undiscovered treasure and he's desperate to know all my secrets.

When he reaches my waist, he peers back up at

me. "I imagined how you'd taste. How your body would writhe and quiver as I made you come with my mouth." He drags his tongue down my stomach, circling my belly button. "Can I do that, Abbey? Can I make you come all over my tongue?"

"God, yes."

I've never been with someone who talked like this. Sure, I've read my fair share of romance novels lately, thanks to Grandma Estelle. I didn't think men like this existed. Now I know they do. And damn if Jude's dirty talk isn't driving me wild with need, an intense craving building inside I don't think will ever be satisfied.

"Good."

His fingers skim along the waistband of my jeans, his eyes never straying from mine as he lowers the zipper. I arch my hips in silent permission, and he eases my jeans and panties down my legs.

For a brief moment, I feel exposed. *Too* exposed. He's still fully dressed and I'm on his bed without a single scrap of clothing on.

"Perfect," he murmurs in appreciation as he pushes my thighs apart. "You are fucking perfect."

Any apprehension I had instantly vanishes, especially when he glides his tongue along my center, sending shivers through my body.

"Oh, god," I whimper, gripping the sheets below me in an attempt to ground myself when I feel like I'm about to lose all control.

"You like that?"

"It's so good." I run my fingers through his hair, digging my nails into his scalp. "You're not even inside me and you feel so good."

"It's killing me not to be," he confesses, pushing a finger inside me, stretching and massaging. "But we have all night. No need to rush things."

"All night? I don't know if I'll last all night."

He peers up at me, my desire coating his lips. "I'll do my best to make sure you do. But first, I need to make sure you come."

He returns his mouth to me, his tongue lapping at my clit as he adds another finger, intensifying the sensation.

"You taste so fucking good, Abbey. Been imagining how you would taste since the day I met you. How you would feel. How you would move."

"Jude," I exhale, his name a plea on my lips.

With each thrust of his fingers and flick of his tongue, my senses are heightened. It's been so long since I've felt anything remotely close to this. I'm not sure how long I'll last.

"What do you need?"

"More. I need more." I circle against him, desperate for release, blind with lust.

"More what?"

"More of your fingers. More of your tongue." I grip his face in my hands, forcing his eyes to mine. "More of you."

"Whatever you need, it's yours." He slides his tongue against my clit, thrusting his fingers in and out of me.

I can't remember the last time Carson did this for me. Whenever we were together, it was about him. After a while, I learned to just fake it so it would be over quicker.

There's no need to fake it with Jude. Not when I feel my body tensing, that familiar sensation bubbling low in my core.

"Don't fight it, Abbey," he says, as if able to read my body. "Let me feel you."

When he gently grazes my clit with his teeth, all my control shatters and I scream his name, waves of euphoria washing over me. He drags out my orgasm, wanting me to experience every sensation, every thrill, every delicious quiver.

When I'm finally sated, he snakes up my body and crushes his mouth against mine, the taste of me on his lips intoxicating.

"What else?" I pant, a renewed wave of bliss cresting inside me when his arousal hits my center.

"What do you mean?"

"What else did you imagine?"

He smirks. "You still want more?"

I crane toward him, taking his earlobe between my teeth. "I'll always want more with you."

My fingers trail down his back, nails digging in as his muscles tense under my touch.

"How the hell do you do that?" He brings his gaze to mine, looking at me in wonder.

"Do what?" I swallow hard.

"Make me lose my mind with just a touch?" He cradles my face in his hands, so much emotion swirling in his dark eyes. "I don't know what I'm supposed to think about this," he confesses. "About you."

My heart squeezes at the confusion and desperation in his words. I wish I had an answer, but I don't.

"Remember what I told you earlier?" I bring my lips back to his. "Don't think. Just feel." I rake my nails down his spine again, eliciting a deep groan from him that sends desire spiraling through me. "Feel me."

I press my mouth back to his, and he swallows my moan as his own. His tongue swipes against mine in an intoxicating combination of affection and lust that ignites every nerve in my body.

Too soon, he breaks away and stands up, hastily shedding his clothes. As he does, I take a moment to appreciate his body. It's not the first time I've seen him shirtless. Hell, I still have fond memories of my first morning here. Of tripping on that last stair and falling into his arms, his body warm and addicting. But seeing him naked... This man belongs in a museum. Sculptors should study him, every inch pure perfection.

Returning to me, he touches his mouth to mine,

his lips moving in a deliberate dance that leaves me sighing.

"This," he murmurs as I relish in the warmth of his chest against mine now that there's nothing between us. "I imagined this."

"Then don't make me wait any longer. We've already waited long enough."

"You're right about that." He reaches for the top drawer of his nightstand and opens it, revealing a stash of condoms.

An unexpected pang of jealousy hits me at the idea that I'm not the only woman he's invited into his bed. We may not have spoken about things in depth, but I've picked up enough from my conversations with Dylan to know he doesn't do the relationship thing. After what he shared earlier, I can't blame him. But I'm not sure how to feel about being just another woman he spends time with before moving on so he doesn't have to get emotionally involved.

So he doesn't have to experience anything remotely resembling pain or heartache.

If I were in his shoes, I wouldn't want to get attached, either.

"Where did you go?"

Jude's voice snaps me back to the present, and I force my gaze to his as he settles between my legs, the condom in place.

"Just thinking," I assure him, pushing down my uneasy thoughts.

"What did we agree on earlier? Don't think." He brings his erection up to me, teasing my entrance. "Just feel." He eases just slightly inside before retreating.

"Jude," I moan, desperation and desire coursing through my veins.

"Please what?" he teases, and I love the playfulness in his tone.

Love that I have this side of Jude back. That we can be these people again. The people we were before I stumbled on that nursery.

"Please put me out of my goddamn misery," I whimper as he continues to torture me, inching inside before pulling back once more.

"You want me to stop?"

"No!" I shout, panic racing through me at the thought.

Chuckling, he brushes his mouth against mine in a barely there kiss that leaves me wanting more. "Then tell me what you want, Abbey."

His voice is gruff, deep, demanding, and I acquiesce to his command.

"I want you to fuck me, Jude."

He's silent for a moment, completely unmoving. Then a conniving smile crawls on his lips.

"Good girl."

I didn't realize two words could have such an effect on me, but hearing him call me a good girl in such a wanton, sensual voice does things to me.

He rewards me by pushing fully inside, taking his time to savor every single inch.

I wrap my arms around him, clinging to his strong body as if he's the only thing anchoring me to this world. We remain motionless for what feels like an eternity, lost in this place of contentment. Of completion. Of unexpected bliss.

"Goddamn," Jude hisses through an intense shiver. "Fucking incredible, Abbey." He slowly pulls back, his eyes meeting mine. "You feel fucking incredible."

With renewed force, he plunges inside again, and I moan at the welcome invasion. Nothing has ever felt this powerful. This mind-blowing. This all-consuming.

Jude buries his head in the crook of my neck, breathing heavily, as if struggling to control himself.

"Let go, Jude," I whisper. "I want you to be free with me. Give me all of you."

He lifts his gaze to mine, a tense silence passing between us. I expect him to remind me he'll never be able to give me all of him. Not when he's still broken into thousands of pieces.

But he doesn't say anything. Instead, he slowly withdraws before thrusting back inside.

This time, he doesn't pause. Doesn't stop. Just fucks me with everything he has.

When his teeth clamp down on my neck, euphoria and agony collide within me, and I cry out. But he doesn't relent. If anything, he fucks me faster. Bites me harder.

There's no doubt in my mind there will be a mark there tomorrow. I like the idea of him marking me, branding me as his. Like the idea of walking past him at the taproom so he can catch a glimpse of all the ways he owned my body tonight.

All the ways he owned me.

As my muscles tighten, my body on the precipice of coming undone once more, I match his movements, thrust for thrust. When he slides his hand between our bodies and rubs my clit, I'm a slave to his touch. An even more intense orgasm bursts inside of me, my cries echoing around us.

"You have no idea how damn good that feels, Abbey. Your pussy clenching around me. It's driving me crazy. I can't…"

He frames my face with his hands, not letting me escape him. Not letting me escape this.

"What the fuck are you doing to me?"

I'm not sure how to take his words. Does he mean in bed? Or in general? So I give him the only answer I can.

"I don't know. But why don't you show me?"

He responds with a primal growl, increasing his speed and intensity until I'm lost in a whirlwind of sensation, each thrust more punishing and desperate. When I'm confident he's going to break me in two, a roar rips through the space, and he jerks through his own release before collapsing on top of me.

Neither one of us moves or says anything for several long moments as we remain a tangled mess of arms and legs. Jude's breaths come in deep, heavy puffs as he tries to regain control.

Finally, he leans in and presses a soft kiss to my nose. "Be right back."

He carefully extricates himself from me and disappears into the en-suite.

Hoping to avoid the awkward situation of him asking me to leave so he can sleep alone, I climb out of his bed and gather my scattered clothing. Just as I'm about to slip on panties, he reappears.

"Where are you going?" he asks with a furrowed brow.

I shrug awkwardly. "Figured you'd want your space."

I start to get dressed, but before I can, he closes the distance between us and grabs my wrist, yanking me against him.

"What I want is to be able to touch you whenever I please throughout the night."

"Are you sure? I don't mind. We don't—"

"I wouldn't say it if I weren't," he interrupts firmly, forcing my eyes to his so I have no choice but to see the sincerity within. "Spend the night with me, Abbey."

I hesitate, contemplating all the reasons this is a

bad idea. But if this is the only night I'll have with him, may as well make it count.

"Okay."

"Okay," he repeats, walking me back to the bed. Once I'm settled under the duvet, he climbs in behind me and wraps me in his embrace.

"I guess you did it," I remark after a few moments of comfortable silence.

"What's that?" he hums sleepily.

"You achieved your goal."

He chuckles, nipping at my shoulder blades. "I did." He forces me onto my back. "But I'm a bit of an overachiever. I'd like to see if I can surpass my goal."

"Is that right?"

"That's right." He runs a hand down my stomach and past my waist, causing my breath to hitch in anticipation.

"In that case," I begin breathlessly. "I'll help you any way I can."

"I was hoping you'd say that." Then he slides a finger back inside me, sending pinpricks of pleasure through my body once more.

# TWENTY-THREE

## *Jude*

A sliver of soft, golden light filters through the curtains in my darkened bedroom, gradually rousing me from a restful sleep. I'm exhausted, but in the best way possible. I haven't felt this satisfied in a long time. This rested. This at peace. All because of Abbey.

Desperate to feel her body against mine, I roll over, expecting her to still be next to me. But when I'm met with cold sheets, I snap my eyes open, confused to learn I'm alone.

Normally, I'd be happy to find my bed empty after spending the night with a woman. But I hate that Abbey's not here. Hate that, despite promising she'd stay, she snuck out anyway.

Or maybe I'm overthinking it. Maybe she needed to use the bathroom.

I slip out of bed and grab a pair of gym shorts from the dresser, tugging them on before heading out of the room. Abbey's door is open so I peek inside, furrowing my brow when I see her duvet is slightly askew, her sheets wrinkled. It was made when I stopped by to grab something yesterday afternoon. And since Abbey was working all day, the only time she would have been able to sleep in the bed was last night.

When did she leave my room? And why?

Even more unsettling, why do I care?

I continue down the stairs, thinking maybe she's doing yoga in the living room or sipping on a coffee in the kitchen — something she usually did in the morning before things became strained. Since then, she's limited the amount of time she's spent outside of her room, at least whenever I've been home.

But she's not down here, either.

She's nowhere.

I don't know why I'm so bothered by her unexpected disappearance. She's free to come and go as she pleases.

But I hate the way it makes me feel.

Needing to clear my mind, I head back upstairs and toss on some running clothes. While some people hate running, I've always enjoyed it. It helps me block out everything else going on in my life and focus solely on putting one foot in front of the other.

But no matter how hard I try to think of anything other than my night with Abbey, she keeps weaseling her way back into my mind. The way she moved, the taste of her lips, the warmth of her skin against mine — it all floods back, leaving me wanting more of her.

Wanting *all* of her.

It's a selfish thought, considering I'm not sure I *can* have all of her.

I'm not sure I *deserve* to have all of her.

A voice that sounds surprisingly like Finn echoes in my head, reminding me I could have her if I would just get over myself and stop worrying about the past repeating itself.

But am I willing to put myself through that again?

Am I *ready* to put myself through that again when I still struggle with the loss?

Hell, the day I found Abbey in the nursery was the first time I'd peeked inside that room in years. We all mourn in our own ways, I suppose. We all handle our grief differently. Whereas I refused to so much as even look at that room, Krista spent nearly every hour of every day in there, crying herself to sleep until all her tears were gone.

Then, one day, she was gone, too.

I fight to push down the memory as I wind my way back down Main Street, skirting by a few locals who are starting their Saturday morning with breakfast at the diner or a cup of coffee at the local café.

And then I see her.

Abbey's sitting at a table outside the coffee shop, leisurely sipping on an iced coffee and reading. Her sunglasses hide her eyes and her blonde hair is styled in a loose braid cascading over her shoulder, most likely hiding the teeth marks I left on her neck last night.

A rush of possessiveness shoots through me from the memory, and before I know what I'm doing, I'm marching up to her, coming to a stop in front of her table.

Sensing my presence, she darts her head up, inhaling sharply when she sees me.

"Jude." She removes her sunglasses. "What are you doing here?" Her eyes dance over my frame as I try to catch my breath. "Are you okay?"

I shake my head, unsure how to respond. This is why I don't get attached. Why I avoid anything serious. I'm all twisted up inside and hate it.

"What are *you* doing here?" I finally ask.

"Having a coffee." She brings the straw back to her mouth. It reminds me of the night we met. How I imagined what her red lips would look like wrapped around my cock.

After last night, I now know.

"There's a coffee machine at home. One that also makes ice coffee."

"It's such a nice morning. I figured I'd come down here and support a local business." She returns her attention to her e-reader, as if we're no one to each other.

As if we didn't spend last night fucking each other until we physically had nothing left.

When I pull out the vacant chair across from her and sit down, she finally looks up from her e-reader. I lean closer so no one can overhear. "Is this because of last night?"

"It has nothing to do with that."

"Are you sure?"

"Of course. Last night was fun, but I'm not naïve, Jude. I know you prefer to keep yourself…unattached. I'm okay with that."

"I don't—"

"It's not a big deal." She reaches across the table and covers my hand with hers. "I didn't sleep with you because I hoped it might turn into something."

Her words sting more than I thought they would. "You didn't?"

It's one thing to set boundaries.

It's another to have them set for you.

"I get it. You're not interested in anything serious. Now that I know what happened, I don't think you *can* be interested in anything serious. Not until you finally come to terms with your past. And that's okay." She assures me without a hint of accusation or incrimination. "I'm only here temporarily anyway, so we don't need to turn last night into more than what it was. Two consenting adults indulging in their cravings. Okay?"

Taking a sip of her coffee, she returns her eyes to her e-reader. I have no idea how she can appear so collected when I want to throw her on the table and have my way with her, especially after hearing her talk about us indulging in our cravings.

This is uncharted territory for me. Usually, I'm the one setting the ground rules. Not because I'm an ass, but because I don't like making promises I can't keep.

But there's something about having this conversation with Abbey that feels inherently wrong.

"So it was just a one-time thing?" I ask in a shaky voice as I fight to mask my emotions over the idea.

"It can be." She shrugs nonchalantly. "Or, I suppose it would technically be a three-time thing in our case."

A blush creeps up her cheeks and she bites down on her bottom lip, obviously remembering the two additional orgasms I gave her throughout the night.

"What I'm trying to say is I don't want you to feel like you owe me anything. We can just go back to the way things were, preferably before things got messy so we can continue our Sunday night bowling tradition. The game's growing on me."

"Is that what you want?" I arch a brow. "To go back to the way things were? Did you not enjoy yourself last night?"

"You know I did," she answers, unable to hide the deepening shade of red on her cheeks.

"So did I. And I think it would be a disservice to deprive ourselves of even more great sex." I drop my voice again, a playful edge sneaking in. "Especially now that we know how incredible we can be together."

"So…what? We'd be friends with benefits? Or roommates with benefits?"

I'm not even sure what kind of arrangement I'm proposing. All I know is that last night with Abbey was unlike anything I've experienced before, and I can't bear the thought of never feeling that again.

Never feeling *her* again.

"Something along those lines," I finally answer. "We're both mature adults and know the score going in. I won't make any promises, and I don't expect you to, either."

"So…just sex," she clarifies.

"Just sex," I confirm, although a small voice in the back of my head warns me this is a disaster waiting to happen. But I can't think about that right now. All I can think about is the memory of Abbey's body trembling beneath me, her nails leaving marks on my skin as I drove into her.

"Okay. Just sex." She extends her hand toward me.

I eye it warily. "What's that for?"

"Shouldn't we shake on it?"

"Perhaps, but I have a better idea."

She arches a brow. "And what's that?"

I push to stand and wrap my hand around hers. When I yank her to her feet and into my body, a gasp escapes her throat.

I curve toward her, able to make out my teeth marks on her neck from last night.

"I think we should fuck on it, Abbey," I growl.

A sinful smile tugs on her lips. "You don't have to ask me twice."

# TWENTY-FOUR

## *Abbey*

"This may have been the best day off I've had in a long time," Jude croons, pulling me into his arms.

I can't help but laugh as I snuggle into him, savoring in the feel of his warm chest.

This has been one of the best days off I've had in a long time, too. Possibly ever. I spent all day in bed with Jude. Or, at least, all day since getting back from the coffee shop.

While I wasn't surprised to see him — considering I'm familiar with his daily routine, including his morning run — I was quite surprised to learn he was upset I snuck out of bed in the middle of the night. I meant what I told him. I was okay if he wanted to keep it a one-time thing.

But after spending all day with him, I realize how crazy I was to think one night would be enough. I've officially lost count of the number of orgasms he's given me over the past few hours. It's as if the man is on a mission to set a world record. And I'll happily go along for the ride.

"I couldn't agree more," I respond lazily as my stomach rumbles. "Although if you expect me to go for round…what is it? Eleven or twelve? I might need to eat something."

"That can be arranged," he says, kissing my nose.

I love when he does that. It may not be sexy, but there's a certain intimacy to it I crave.

"Is there anywhere open this late?" I ask after glancing at the clock on his nightstand to see it's already after nine.

"Not really." He slips out of bed and walks toward the dresser.

"Then where will we order takeout from?" I roll onto my side and prop my head in my hand, admiring his ass. My god, the man is chiseled perfection.

"We're not ordering takeout," he declares as he tugs on a pair of gray sweatpants.

"But—"

"I'll cook."

"You…cook?"

Despite living together for over two months now, I've yet to see him cook. Then again, he hasn't been home much these past few weeks. Neither have I.

After tugging on a t-shirt, he returns to me, his lips hovering over mine. "I'm full of surprises."

"I'm beginning to realize that," I exhale as he presses his mouth more firmly against mine.

"You have time for a shower if you want," he says, pulling back. "Is there anything you won't eat or are allergic to?"

"Nope. I'm easy."

A devilish glint flashes in his eyes as he slides his hand between my legs, teasing me. "And I love that about you."

He gives me one last kiss, then retreats, leaving me somewhat frustrated and contemplating going into my bedroom to take care of the problem myself.

But I like the idea of Jude owning all my orgasms. At least for now.

Climbing out of his bed, I pad on light feet across the hallway into my room to take a much-needed shower. The warm water is invigorating on my body, my muscles aching from the past twenty-four hours. One thing is certain. I may need to increase the intensity of my yoga workouts if I'm to keep up with Jude. The man is a damn machine.

And I'm enjoying every second of it.

After toweling off and piling my curls on the top of my head with a silk scrunchie, I rummage through my dresser for something clean. Unfortunately, I haven't done laundry lately. I was planning on doing it today, but I never got around to it. All I have is one pair of clean underwear. Nothing else. I could throw on something dirty, but I decide to borrow some of Jude's clothes instead.

Making my way back to his room, I open the middle drawer of his dresser and find the t-shirt I slept in my first night here. After slipping it on, I head downstairs, the aroma of garlic and onion growing stronger with every step.

As I emerge into the kitchen, Jude looks up from stirring something on the stove, his eyes flaming at the sight of me.

"I hope you don't mind that I borrowed one of your shirts. I hoped to do laundry today, but someone couldn't stop putting his dick in me."

"I didn't hear any complaints." He chews on his bottom lip as his heated gaze drinks me in, a quiver working its way through me.

"And you won't." I saunter into the kitchen, leaning against the island. "You can stick your dick in me anytime you want."

"I might have to take you up on that rather generous offer." Closing the distance between us, he touches his lips to mine, taking me somewhat by surprise.

I had this image in my mind of keeping anything sexual or intimate in the bedroom only. Thought when we were outside the bedroom, it would be business as usual.

I'm starting to think nothing about this arrangement will be business as usual.

"Wine?" Jude asks, gradually pulling back.

"What? No beer?"

"While I love beer, I think chardonnay would pair better with what I'm making."

"What's that?"

"Mushroom risotto with salmon."

I let out a low whistle. "And here I thought you were just going to throw some pasta in boiling water and open a jar of sauce."

He grimaces at the notion.

"First, my mother would disown me if I ever used jarred sauce. She'd go on and on about my *nonna* and *bisnonna* coming back from the dead to lash me with a wet noodle or beat me with a wooden spoon. Or something equally dramatic."

"I take it you're part Italian then."

"On my mom's side." He pours us each a glass of golden chardonnay and hands one to me, a playful glint in his eye. "Second, you're going to need your energy for what I have planned for you later, and pasta with jarred sauce won't cut it."

"I like the sound of that."

"Me, too. Cheers."

"Cheers." I touch my glass to his, then take a sip, savoring the smooth flavor of the oaky chardonnay. "Do you need help with anything?"

"I have it all under control. Just have a seat and relax. Dinner will be ready soon."

"Okay." I hoist myself onto one of the stools by the island, watching him move around the kitchen with ease.

There's something about a man who knows his way around the kitchen that is inherently attractive, especially as he tastes the food before adding a few seasonings. It's obvious he's extremely comfortable cooking. And without a recipe, too.

"How did you learn to cook?" I ask after watching him for several minutes. "Not that I'm complaining since I get to reap the benefits. But I haven't met many men who could cook macaroni and cheese without destroying it, let alone mushroom risotto with salmon."

He brings his wine to his lips and takes a sip. "It was kind of out of necessity, actually. Right after Krista and I were married, she twisted her leg up pretty badly in a skiing accident. Tore her ACL and everything. She was on crutches for months while she recovered. And since takeout food and Ramen noodles would get old fairly quickly, I decided to learn how to cook. At first, I was fucking terrible." He laughs under his breath, a nostalgic gleam in his gaze.

To be honest, I'm surprised he's talking about this, all things considered.

Maybe this is what he needs, though. To finally talk about his time with Krista.

Just like I needed to talk about Carson. My dad. My mom.

"You'd think since I knew how to brew beer I'd be able to do this no problem, but I sucked at it. The first meal I attempted was baked chicken thighs. Simple enough, right?"

"I would say so," I agree.

"Well, turns out I bought the wrong kind of thighs — boneless instead of bone-in. Not that big of a deal, except I didn't adjust the cooking time accordingly, so they turned out rubbery and chewy. And don't even get me started on the rice." He shakes his head with a self-deprecating smile. "I put in way too much liquid, and it came out mushy. But Krista…" He peers into the distance for a moment. "She was so good about it. You can tell she didn't enjoy it, but she still ate everything because she didn't want to hurt my feelings."

I don't immediately say anything. I'm not sure *what* to say. It feels strange listening to him talk about his ex-wife, especially when I can still feel her presence in this house.

"Well, it looks like you've learned a bit since then," I finally remark.

"I have." He nods, though there's a hint of sadness in his gaze. Then he clears his throat. "How about you? Where did you pick up your cooking skills? I may have snuck a few bites of those breakfast potatoes you made your first morning here."

"I figured." I wink, taking a sip of my wine. "I

guess I learned out of necessity, too. Even before my mom dropped me off with my dad, she wasn't around much and I was often left to fend for myself, especially after my grandmother died when I was seven. Before that, she practically raised me. When she died, it was just my mom."

His expression falls. "I'm sorry. I didn't mean to—"

"It's okay. It is what it is. You can't change the past, but you can take charge of your future."

"Is that what you're doing?" He arches a brow. "Taking charge of your future?"

"I'd like to think so."

"And what does the future look like for you?" He asks as he carries two plates to the island, setting one in front of me before assuming the chair beside me.

"How far are we talking?"

His brows pull in as a brief moment of contemplation covers his face. It reminds me of the concentration he exhibits when brewing beer.

And when thrusting inside me.

"How about one, five, and ten years?"

I snap out of my inappropriate thoughts and take a bite of risotto. As the creamy flavor dances on my tongue, I release a satisfied moan.

"Watch it," Jude warns, leaning toward me. "Or I'll throw you on the island and make you really moan. To hell with how hungry you are." His eyes lock with mine, dark and full of lust as they trace over my mouth. "Because I'm famished for something else to eat."

"You just had me. All day."

"There's no such thing as too much of a good thing, Abbey. And you?" He brushes his lips against mine. "You are most definitely a good thing."

I whimper at the feel of him, doing everything to remind myself this isn't real. He can say all the right things, but it won't change who he is.

Won't change his past.

Won't change that whatever this is between us will never be anything more than what it is right now.

"Let me hear it." He pulls back, as if he didn't just turn me into mush. "One, five, and ten."

"Right."

I snap back to the present, giving his question serious consideration.

After swallowing a bite of salmon, I say, "One year from now, I'd like to be settled in my own place with a stable job, preferably back in the nonprofit sector. Not that I'm not grateful for your help in giving me a job and a place to stay," I add quickly. "Especially now with the added…perks."

"I quite enjoy the added perks, too." He grazes his hand up my thigh, and I part my legs for him, but he draws back at the last second.

"Tease."

"Maybe." He waggles his brows. "How about in five years?"

"I'd like to be in a healthy relationship. I still want to find love, even if you think it's bullshit."

"I don't think it's bullshit. I just…"

"You don't want that," I finish.

He doesn't say anything, but I notice a flicker of something in his eyes, as if he's about to correct me. But he doesn't.

Instead, he presses on. "And in ten years?"

"Have a family. Have a job I enjoy. Be one of those couples that make their kids cringe at how much they can't keep their hands off each other, even after being married forever."

The corners of my mouth curve up as I imagine this future for me. But its tinged in sadness, too. Because Jude won't be a part of it.

"I hope you get everything you want. If anyone deserves it, it's you."

I want to tell him he deserves all of these things, too. That he deserves to find happiness and not be weighed down by his past.

But some lessons in life can't be taught or forced down your throat. You have to learn them on your own.

And this is one lesson Jude has to learn for himself.

That he needs to *want* for himself.

I can't do it for him.

# TWENTY-FIVE

## *Jude*

Sunshine warms my face as I sit in the back yard of my mom's house, everyone relaxing after a filling Sunday dinner. Except for the kids. They never seem to stop. Beckham's often joked that Maggie, his stepdaughter, has two speeds — full on or dead stop. I believe it. Even so, Abbey's right there with all of them, pushing little Jeremiah on the baby swing as Presley and Maggie climb the rock wall attached to the playscape.

I saw how great she was with the kids when I brought her here for her first Second Sunday. But that was before I knew her well. Now that I've gotten to know her quite intimately over the past few weeks, I see something I didn't back then.

Despite all the people who've abandoned her

throughout her life, she's still full of so much hope. So much damn love. She deserves to share that love with other people.

Something tightens in my chest at the thought.

"You're staring hard enough that you're about to burn a hole in her."

When Finn's voice cuts through, I jerk my gaze away from Abbey. My younger brother grins like the bastard he is, leaning back in the chair across from me with a knowing look.

"I'm not staring," I mutter, taking a quick sip of my beer to cover my reaction, heat creeping up the back of my neck.

"Oh, sure," Beckham jumps in from his spot on the wicker couch. "Because that wasn't the most lovesick expression I've ever seen."

"Lovesick?" I nearly choke on the word. "You guys are out of your minds."

"Pretty sure that's an 'I'm getting laid and loving it' smile," Finn teases. "What do you think, Beck?"

"Definitely getting laid," my older brother agrees, although he's only older by less than a year.

It's probably why Beckham, Finn, and I have always gotten along so well. There's only a little more than two years difference in age between the three of us, with Hayden being eight years older than me and Dylan being five years younger.

"The only question is by who?"

"Whom," Finn corrects. "The proper question is getting laid by *whom*?"

"When the fuck did you become the grammar police?" Beckham shoots back before waggling his brows. "Or is it because you're trying to impress a certain librarian?"

"How many times do I have to tell you? Genevieve is just a friend." Finn purposefully avoids our gaze as he takes another swig of beer. "This isn't about me anyway. This is about Jude."

"Is your sex life that boring that you need to pry into mine?"

"So you admit you're having sex?" Finn beams.

I open my mouth to protest, then shake my head. It's useless. My brothers know me better than anyone. Know when I'm upset. When I'm struggling. And, as they've already demonstrated, when I'm happy.

Abbey definitely makes me happy.

I felt it that very first night. She has this infectious enthusiasm for life, even when it's beaten her down, and I can't help but be attracted to her.

I shift my eyes toward her, watching as she politely extricates herself from the kids and makes her way toward the house.

"Fuck off," I say, getting to my feet and starting in the same direction.

"Where are you going, lover boy?" Beckham calls after me, grinning like he knows something I don't.

"None of your business."

Finn chimes in with a low whistle. "Gotta say, Jude, not sure I've ever seen you this pussy-whipped. Didn't know you had it in you."

I flip them both off as I make my way into the house. Their laughter follows me, but I push it out of my head. I'm not about to give them the satisfaction of teasing me about Abbey — not when we're just having some fun.

Nothing more.

I find her in the living room, looking at an old family photo placed on the mantle. She doesn't notice me at first, but when she does, she smiles, soft and easy. It does something to me every damn time.

"Everything okay?" I step closer.

"I got distracted on my way to fill up my wine." She holds up her glass before returning her attention to the picture. "I love all the photos your mom has. It makes this place feel like a home." She peers into the distance, a look of contemplation crossing her brow. "I don't think my parents ever displayed a single photo of me."

My heart squeezes at the notion. What must it have felt like for her to be raised by people like that? I couldn't imagine.

"Come on." I take her glass and set it on a nearby side table, linking my fingers with hers. "There's something I want to show you."

Her eyebrows lift, but she doesn't hesitate. I lead her down the hall, past the kitchen, and into the garage. It's cool and dark, the air carrying a faint scent of old wood and dust.

With a flick of a switch, warm light floods the space. Abbey steps inside, her eyes wide as she takes it all in. Along one wall is a small bar, stocked with all sorts of liquor and glasses. Beyond that are three small stainless steel tanks — my dad's old brewing setup. While I could have replaced them with a system that has more automations, I don't want to do that until I have to.

My dad used this equipment. I want to continue using it as long as I possibly can, even if it requires me to be more hands on during the brewing process.

"This is where it all started," I say, gesturing at the tanks. "My dad used to spend hours out here, brewing beer, talking about opening his own brewery someday. That dream died when he did, but I like knowing I can keep some part of him alive, even if it's through beer."

"I think that's sweet." Abbey moves closer to the bar, running her fingers over the worn wood. Along the counter are photos — my parents on their wedding day, Finn and Beckham as kids, me holding Dylan, Hayden and my dad laughing over a bottle of beer. Memories, each one of them.

Abbey picks up a photo of me as a teenager standing next to my dad in this very room. "Is this you?"

"That was the first time I helped him brew." I

swallow hard. "He was already getting sick and having trouble doing simple tasks, so he asked me to help him. But I had no idea what I was doing, so I let the wort temperature get too low and didn't sparge the water correctly."

"I have no idea what any of that means," Abbey says with a laugh.

I run a hand through my hair. "At the time, neither did I. But my dad didn't care that I completely messed up his beer. He said it was more about spending time together."

Abbey nods, setting the picture back down before turning her gaze toward me. "Tell me your favorite memory of him."

The request catches me off guard. It's not something I talk about often, not something I let myself dwell on. But with her, everything's a little easier.

Leaning against the bar, I cross my arms and think back. "He used to take me camping. He'd always try to find an activity to do with each of us so we could have some one-on-one time with him, and for me, it was camping. I always loved being outdoors. We'd stay up late, sit by the fire, and talk about everything, especially as I got older and more mature. Life. Love. The future. I don't even remember half of what we said, but I remember the way it felt. Like nothing else in the world mattered except that moment."

"That sounds perfect," she whispers.

"It was." I pause, feeling the weight of the

memory, the pull of something deeper. "I haven't thought about it in a long time."

A heavy silence hangs between us, the kind that's charged with meaning. Abbey moves closer, radiating warmth.

"Thanks for sharing that with me," she says softly, reaching up to brush her fingers against my face. It's a subtle touch, but it sends a current through me, something I can't ignore.

"I didn't mean to get all heavy on you," I say, trying to lighten the mood, but my voice comes out rougher than I intended.

Abbey shakes her head, her gaze never leaving mine. "I don't mind. I like seeing this side of you."

And that's the problem. She's seeing too much. Making me feel things I swore I wouldn't let myself feel again.

But with her so close, her eyes soft and full of something I can't name, I don't care. I just want her. Here. Now. To hell with all the reasons this is a bad idea.

I hook an arm around her waist and tug her closer as my eyes drink in every line of her face. Her brilliant blue eyes. Her pink cheeks. Her full lips. I've never met anyone so damn beautiful. And she's mine. For now.

Unable to go another second without feeling her, I crash my lips against hers, hungry and demanding.

Relief floods through me as I relish in her taste, her tongue tangling with mine.

The past few hours were pure torture, knowing she was within reach, but I couldn't have her. Couldn't do what I really wanted. What I've been craving since she slipped out of my bed this morning.

Now I can.

And I can't wait any longer.

Deepening the exchange, I hoist her up and set her onto the bar. As I trail my hand up the inside of her thigh, I savor in the feel of her smooth skin under my fingertips. Her skirt offers little resistance, and I inch higher, reaching the edge of her panties.

"Jude," she exhales, pulling away from my mouth. She takes a moment to catch her breath, her lust-filled eyes locking with mine. "What are you doing?"

"I need you, Abbey." I curve toward her, capturing her lips in another rough kiss. "Been desperate for you all damn day."

I push aside her panties, revealing how wet she already is for me.

"Do you have any idea how hard it's been to look but not touch, especially after spending all night touching?" I murmur against her neck, planting kisses on her skin as I tease her clit with my thumb.

"All night feeling." I slide a finger inside of her, savoring in her tightness and warmth. "All night fucking."

When I add another finger and start thrusting

faster, she releases a cry. I cover her mouth with mine, swallowing her moans. "I need to have you," I confess, my motions getting more hurried and desperate. "Don't make me wait any longer."

"Then have me," she pants, her chest heaving through her growing labored breaths. "I'm yours."

"Mine," I growl, a rush of possessiveness burning inside of me.

"Yours."

Pulling back slightly, I reach into my pocket and retrieve a condom from my wallet.

"Was this your plan all along, Mr. Lawrence?" she teases, and damn if hearing her sultry voice address me like that doesn't make me harden even more.

"And if it was, Ms. Rhodes?" I lower the zipper on my jeans.

"Then I'm more than happy to go along for the ride… If you know what I mean." She waggles her brows.

"I most certainly do," I say, bringing my erection up to her, her warmth surrounding me.

When I thrust into her, she parts her lips, a scream begging to be set free, but I muffle the sound with my hand. "Quiet."

"Stop fucking me so good and I won't be so loud," she says once I uncover her mouth.

"Never, Abbey." I bury my head in the crook of her neck, nipping at her skin. "I'll never stop giving you what you need."

"Oh, god," she whimpers as I drive into her harder and harder, wild with lust.

This is reckless. We agreed to keep whatever this is just between us. There's no need to announce ourselves to the world, considering it's just sex. Not to mention, I'm her boss.

But with every day I spend around her, with every part of me I reveal to her, I'm beginning to think it's not just sex. That it never could be just sex.

And the thought petrifies me.

But not enough to walk away.

# TWENTY-SIX

## *Abbey*

"Is it obvious I was just railed by my boss?" I ask as I peer at my reflection in the mirror, attempting to tame my hair.

My curls have a mind of their own on a good day.

After Jude's gotten a hold of me, it's usually a lost cause.

In my defense, I didn't expect for him to lock the door to his office and slam me against the wall when I stopped by to store my purse before starting my shift.

Although, I shouldn't be all that surprised. It's not the first time he's done this.

At first, we kept all overt displays of affection confined to his house. That only lasted so long before temptation got the better of us. It doesn't matter that we spend our nights tangled up with each other, going at it until neither one of us has anything left. I still need more of him.

I fear I'll *always* need more of him.

"I don't care if it is," Jude whispers against my neck as he approaches from behind. He presses a hand to my stomach, pulling me closer as his lips trail along my skin, leaving fire in their wake. "That way, any of those guys out there who check out your ass will know it belongs to me."

He slides his hand along the curve of my frame, cupping my ass possessively. Then he lifts my denim skirt, shifting my panties to the side and sliding a finger along my clit.

"So does this delicious pussy."

My eyes flutter closed, and I moan, leaning my head against his chest as he turns me into putty with his talented fingers.

"You're going to make me late for my shift," I murmur, trying to keep my head on straight when I feel like I'm losing more and more control every day.

"And you don't want to be late." His voice is low and seductive, causing a maddening need to seep into my veins. "I hear your boss can be quite the hard ass."

"You have no idea," I playfully groan. "The man is insufferable."

He pulls his hand away and lands a hard smack on my ass.

I yelp, then whimper as he rubs the flesh. "I'll

show you how insufferable I can be." He nips at my neck.

"Is that a threat? Or a promise?"

He spins me around, his lips hovering over mine. "You'll find out later. I have plans for you."

I drape my arm over his shoulder, toying with a few tendrils of his hair. "What kind of plans?"

"I wouldn't want to ruin the surprise, but they involve me…" He touches a kiss to one corner of my mouth before moving to the other side. "And you." He pulls back slightly, mischief glinting in his eyes. "And absolutely no clothes."

"I like the sound of that."

"Me, too." He covers my mouth, his tongue swiping against mine in a way that makes me want to stay with him forever.

But I can't.

Reluctantly pushing away, I give him one last heated look before turning from him.

I'm about to disappear into the taproom when the tiny hairs all over my body stand on end, a shiver trickling down my spine.

Glancing behind me, I'm not surprised to find Jude leaning against the doorjamb of his office, his arms crossed over his chest, causing his t-shirt to stretch around his muscular frame. His eyes are trained on me like he's gone hungry for days and I'm the first source of sustenance he's encountered. It makes my core clench, desire pooling low in my belly.

If I weren't already late, I would haul him back into his office. Then again, if there's one thing Jude's taught me over the past several weeks, it's that delayed gratification can make it all worth it.

"Did you get lost?" Lindsey teases when I pass her on my way to the bar. "You were back there for quite a while."

Slipping behind the counter, I turn on the sink and wash my hands, glancing at my watch. "I'm not that late. My shift only started a few minutes ago."

"Mmm hmm." She gives me a knowing grin as she joins me behind the bar, grabbing a glass and placing it beneath a tap. "No wonder boss man's been less of a hard ass lately. He's getting laid."

"I don't know what you're talking about." I keep my eyes trained forward, hoping she can't see the blush creeping up my face.

Or the scratches on my neck from where Jude's unshaven jawline scraped against my sensitive skin as he thrust inside me.

"I'm not blind," Lindsey responds. "I see the way he looks at you. We all do. He's got it bad."

I fully face her. "It's not like—"

"It's okay. Your secret's safe with me."

I part my lips, about to argue it's not what she thinks. Instead, I blow out a breath. "Are we that obvious?"

"Only a little." With a wink, she heads back out to the patio to drop off the beer she just poured.

After checking to see all the prep work has already been done, I grab the disinfectant spray and a towel, wiping down the tables in preparation for the evening rush. I need to do something to distract myself from Jude's looming presence in my life.

And Lindsey's statement that he's got it bad for me.

He wasn't supposed to have it bad. Either was I. But I'm in deep and I'm not sure how to dig myself out now.

I'm not sure I want to.

"Abbey. Is that you?"

I snap my head up, my expression widening when I see one of my closest friends from my Peace Corps days approaching.

"Becca?" I all but shriek, dropping my dishtowel and throwing my arms around her, giving her a tight hug. "What are you doing here?" I pull back.

"A family friend is getting married in Tahoe this weekend, and everyone says this place has the best beer this side of the Mississippi. I had to come check it out for myself. Never in a million years did I think I'd run into you!" She beams as she clutches my hands. "How are you? You look…happy."

"I am happy," I say without a single ounce of hesitation.

This is the happiest I've been in a while. Maybe ever.

I've lived most of my life anticipating what's next.

I've never been content to just enjoy the moment. To just be.

Lately, that's all I've been doing… Enjoying the moment. It's been amazing for my soul. Exactly what I needed after Carson.

"I've actually been meaning to reach out, but life's been crazy lately. When I got your email about job leads a month or so ago, I didn't respond because I wasn't in a position to help, but I am now."

I furrow my brow. "What do you mean?"

"I recently started working for Ever Clear Industries as their social responsibility manager."

"Ever Clear?" I respond, searching my mind to place the name. Then it clicks. They're a huge food conglomerate. Even so, I've been around long enough to know that many of these huge corporations have an entire department dedicated to improving their image through social responsibility projects.

"I know. I know. I went to the dark side." She laughs. "But let's be real. At some point, we all need to make a living. And working for Ever Clear allows me to do that while still making a positive impact."

I can't argue with that, especially knowing how highly sought after someone with Becca's skills and experience would be. During our time together in Zambia, she was a natural leader and mentor to many of us newer volunteers, guiding us through the challenges of acclimating to a different culture and way of life.

"I have a pretty good team, but most of them came up in the corporate world. No one with the kind of background you have. Their experience with social responsibility is what they've read in a book or learned during college classes. There's not a single Peace Corps alumni amongst them."

"Okay…," I draw out, somewhat uneasy about where this is going.

"I was planning on reaching out to you after the weekend to see if you were interested in coming to work with me. But here you are. It's like kismet."

I blink repeatedly. "You want me to come work at Ever Clear?"

"I get it. They're supposedly the big bad wolf, but they *are* doing good work. Part of my role is making sure all of their projects align with sustainable practices, environmental responsibility, and community impact. My team is in charge of several initiatives to bring clean water to rural communities all over the globe, as well as educating women on the importance of clean water. As you know, clean water disproportionately affects women in many lesser developed countries."

I nod, all too familiar with the issue facing many of these countries. During my time in the Peace Corps, my focus was on working with women, teaching them ways to enact change in the hopes of decreasing infant mortality rates.

"The pay would easily be four times what you made at AquaPath."

I all but choke on my saliva. Four times what I made at my last nonprofit job? That's more than I thought I'd ever make. Hell, it's more than Carson made at the finance firm.

"I know you said in your email you were looking for something in the nonprofit sector, but you can still make a difference, even when working for a larger corporation."

I let her words sink in, my mind racing with possibilities. I've been searching for a job, a way to finally stand on my own without relying on anyone else. As grateful as I am to Jude for everything he's done for me, the truth remains… I still need his help to stay above water.

But the job Becca's offering would give me the one thing I've craved all my life — true independence.

"Where would I work from?" I ask, wanting to get all the information before I agree.

"As I'm sure you're aware, there will be a great deal of international travel involved. But when you're stateside, you'll be based out of New York."

"Wow. That's…far."

"Don't worry. The company offers relocation reimbursement and can even put you up in one of their corporate apartments while you find something more permanent."

I nod slowly, taking it all in. "I see."

"I understand I've thrown a lot at you, and while you're working." She waves her hand around at the taproom. "Take some time to think about it. But promise you will consider it, Abbey. I said it when we met all those years ago. And I'll say it again. You're meant to do big things."

"Yeah," I say noncommittally. "Maybe so. When do you need an answer?"

"As soon as possible. We're slated to start a new program in Zambia in the beginning of September."

"Zambia?"

She nods. "Near the village where you lived and worked during your Peace Corps assignment. Told you. This job is perfect for you."

She briefly looks away, holding up two fingers to a few other women waiting near the door, presumably some of the friends she's visiting.

"You'll let me know?" she asks, returning her eyes to mine.

"Of course." I force a smile despite the uncertainty swirling in my mind. "It was good seeing you."

"You, too." She gives me a tight squeeze. "Hope to see much more of you soon."

She releases me and I watch her leave, staring into space as I consider whether I can take her up on her offer.

If she approached me a month ago, I wouldn't have hesitated. I would have jumped at this opportunity.

That was before I spent time in Sycamore Falls.

Before I got to know Jude.

Before I felt the one thing I've been searching for as long as I can remember…

A place to belong.

Can I give that up for a high-paying job?

Can I walk away from Jude?

# TWENTY-SEVEN

### *Abbey*

"What are you going to do?" Dylan asks as I sit across from her at a table in the lounge of the Inn at Holley Ridge, which seems to be what Sycamore Falls is most famous for — an expansive property on a lake with a gorgeous resort and wedding facility.

And home to the famous Holley Ridge Christmas Festival.

Now that the inn is officially open for business again after extensive renovations, this is where we've been having our book club meetings, since Parker, one of the other women in the book club, owns the inn.

I never thought I'd be the type of person to be in a book club, but this group has blown all my preconceived notions to pieces, considering each book seems to be even spicier than the one before.

I've certainly been enjoying these books.

And Jude's definitely been reaping the benefits.

But for how much longer?

That question has been plaguing me since my run-in with Becca yesterday. And when I walked into the lobby of Holley Ridge less than an hour ago, everyone in the book club picked up on the fact that something was bothering me. Which is why I've spent the past several minutes telling them everything. About my arrangement with Jude. About my growing feelings. And about this once-in-a-lifetime job offer that will require me to move three thousand miles away.

"I have no idea," I answer honestly, playing with the stem of my wineglass filled with chardonnay — my drink of choice for book club.

"What's holding you back?" Haley, Beckham's wife, leans closer, her auburn hair cascading over her shoulder.

"I think we know precisely what that is." Dylan waggles her brows. "Or perhaps I should say who."

I don't even try to deny it. Not now that I've finally spilled the beans about our secret arrangement. Although no one seemed surprised to learn we've been sleeping together.

"Have you told him about the job?" she asks.

I slowly shake my head. "Not yet."

"Why not?"

"I'm worried about how he'll react." I tap my nails nervously against the wood table. "Or more appropriately, how he *doesn't* react."

Parker tilts her head. "How so?"

"I'm worried he won't seem fazed by the thought of me leaving. And I get it," I add quickly. "It's stupid. We agreed it was just sex. Hell, *I'm* the one who suggested it just be sex."

"But did you do that because that's what you want?" Dylan raises a pointed brow. "Or because that's what you knew *Jude* would want?"

I open my mouth to protest, but snap it shut, her words hitting a little too close to home.

I may have only known Dylan a few months, but between working together a couple of days a week as well as spending time together outside of the taproom, we've gotten to know each other fairly well. It shouldn't surprise me that she picked up on my tendency to sacrifice my needs just to avoid being rejected.

Hell, that's how I ended up completely dependent on Carson in the first place. I was petrified I'd lose him. But after shit hit the fan on our wedding day, I swore I'd never willingly put myself in that position again.

But isn't that what I'm doing by even entertaining the possibility of turning down Becca's job offer?

"It doesn't matter," I finally say, my voice firm.

"I'm more than aware of his reluctance to date, especially after I learned about…everything. A few weeks of sex won't change his mind."

"Never underestimate the power of the magical pussy," Grandma Estelle remarks.

I choke back my laugh at her blunt response. I doubt I'll ever get used to some of the things that come out of this woman's mouth. Most eighty-plus-year-old women I've met have been reserved.

Not Grandma Estelle.

And I couldn't imagine her being any other way.

"As much as I'd love to believe in the power of the magical pussy, like in this book…" I lift my e-reader for emphasis, "that's just not real life. There are no fairy tales. No white knight coming to save the day."

"I'm going to preface this by saying I hate this conversation since it involves my brother," Dylan begins with a hint of feigned disgust, "but I've seen you together. I've seen the way he looks at you, Abbey." She gives me a sincere smile. "I don't think it's just sex for him. I don't think it's *ever* been just sex for him. He's just too stubborn to admit it."

"Lawrence men and their damn stubbornness," Haley remarks under her breath with a dramatic roll of her eyes.

"It's a family trait." Dylan smirks at her before turning back to me. "Which is exactly why you need to talk to him."

"I know I need to tell him about the job eventually, especially if I take it."

"If?" Parker interjects. "This is a great opportunity, right?"

"It is. I'm just trying to figure out if it's the right opportunity for me."

"Let me ask you something," Grandma Estelle chimes in. "Take Jude out of the equation. If you never met him, would you take the job?"

"Without a doubt," I answer quickly.

"Then I think you know what you need to do." Dylan reaches across the table and gives my hand a squeeze. "Be honest with him. Tell him the truth. That you have this amazing opportunity but the only thing holding you back is how you feel about him. Because you love him."

I part my lips, about to argue I'm not in love with him, but it's useless. I've always been a horrible liar anyway.

"I didn't mean for this to happen," I admit through the tightness in my throat, the reality of everything sinking in. It feels like an impossible situation.

"No one ever does, sweetie," Grandma Estelle offers. "That's the scary thing about love. It hits you when you least expect it and sinks its claws into you until you have no choice but to declare defeat."

"Regardless of what you decide about the job…,"

Parker adds, "You deserve to tell him how you feel. Not for him, but for you. So you won't always have to wonder. So you can start the next chapter of your life with a clean slate. Whether it's here with Jude or in New York."

I stare straight ahead, considering her words. She has a point. If I take this job without mentioning anything to him, I'll leave unfinished business behind. I'll never truly be able to move on.

But is *he* finally ready to move on? I'm not sure if he can, the memory of his raw heartache the day he found me in the nursery still fresh in my mind.

"I went through something similar with Callum," Parker continues. "He swore off love after being betrayed pretty badly. Made it clear he could never give me anything more than a no-strings fling. I took a risk and told him I wanted more after realizing I'd fallen in love with him, even though I fought it. Now I can't picture my life without him in it."

"And if Jude rejects me?" I ask, my voice barely above a whisper. "If he can't give me more?"

Parker gives me an understanding look. "It's a risk you have to take."

I'm no stranger to rejection by any means.

All my life, I've been rejected and tossed aside. First, by my mom. Then my dad. Most recently, by Carson.

But the idea of Jude rejecting me stings worse

than I thought possible. With him, I've finally found a place where I belong.

A place to call home.

The idea of losing all of that guts me.

# TWENTY-EIGHT

## *Jude*

"What's going on here?" Abbey remarks as she walks into the house after getting home from her book club meeting. "I thought you were going to work late in the brewhouse."

"I was." I wipe my hands on a dishtowel and turn toward her, pulling her against me. "But I hated the idea of you being all alone in my bed with no one to keep you warm." I feather my lips against hers.

At one point, I spent all my free time in the brewhouse. I didn't want to be home any more than necessary. The memories that lingered in this place were too painful to bear.

Then Abbey walked into my life.

Now, I'm able to find a modicum of comfort within the walls of my house.

Thanks to Abbey.

"Remind me never to give you a day off again. I don't care if it's for book club. I love having you nearby."

She smiles, but there's tension behind it. It's not her usual carefree, enigmatic smile that sends my pulse racing.

"What are you making?" She pushes out of my hold. "It smells delicious."

I try not to read too much into her demeanor, but I can't shake the feeling that something's going on. She's been distracted all day. I want to call her out on it, press her about what's bothering her, but I'm not sure we have that kind of relationship. Actually, I *know* we don't. Or we're not supposed to.

Lately, I've been questioning who we are to each other more and more. Who I *want* to be to her.

"Pork tenderloin. Is that okay?"

She stands on her tiptoes and drapes an arm along my neck, her playful side returning. "You spoil me. You're going to make it hard to—" She stops short, inhaling a sharp breath.

That unsettled feeling intensifies, my stomach hardening. "To what?"

She parts her lips, her eyes searching mine as she struggles to find the right words.

"I'm going to make it hard to…what, Abbey?" I prod, my pulse increasing with every second she remains silent.

Finally, she blows out a long breath and steps out of my embrace. "Someone came into the taproom yesterday."

"Who?"

"An old friend from my time in the Peace Corps."

"Okay…," I draw out, unsure where this is going. Why she kept this from me.

Did she, though? It's not like we have the type of relationship where we share things with each other.

We don't have a relationship. Period.

"Now she works for a big food conglomerate as the social responsibility manager."

"Social responsibility manager?" I repeat, clueless about what that is.

"A lot of big corporations have entire departments devoted solely to social responsibility. The goal is to develop a positive social value for the company and give back to various communities."

"What does that have to do with you?"

She gives me a sheepish smile. "She offered me a place on her team."

My expression widens and, without hesitation, I wrap her in my arms, swinging her around. "That's amazing, Abbey."

"Yeah," she says, but her voice lacks even a hint of enthusiasm.

Confusion knits my brow as I set her back on her feet. "Why aren't you happy?"

"I should be. It's a great job with an incredible

salary. I wouldn't have to depend on anyone in order to pay my bills, which is what I've wanted since I walked out on Carson and realized just how much control I'd unknowingly given him over my life."

"Then what's the problem?"

"It's in New York."

"Oh." I swallow hard, neither of us saying anything for several long moments.

She doesn't have to. I already know what she's thinking. It's written all over her face.

She wants me to give her a reason to stay.

But I can't do that.

"You shouldn't let that hold you back, Abbey," I tell her, trying to sound supportive but feeling like I'm choking on my own words. "Don't give up this opportunity for anything…" A painful lump forms in my throat. Almost as if my body is fighting against what I'm about to say. "Or anyone."

I give her a pointed stare, everything I've left unspoken hanging heavy between us.

"I just thought—"

"We both knew this had an expiration date when it started," I interrupt before she can finish. "Now we know when that is." I force a smile, my voice trembling slightly as my true emotions fight to seep through the cracks. "I'll definitely miss having you around…"

"Just not enough to—"

"No," I declare firmly, not wanting to make this any harder than it already is.

She doesn't say anything for several long moments. Just stares at me. Finally, she closes her eyes, releasing a shuttering breath. "I understand."

When she returns her gaze to mine, a faint smile plays at the corners of her lips, as if I didn't just rip out her heart and shatter it into a million pieces all over the kitchen floor.

"I guess we should probably make the most out of the time we have left."

She saunters up to me with a confident stride, but I can see the hurt in her eyes, despite her brave front. Just like the night she walked into my bar in a wedding dress.

"Unless you just want to call it quits now," she adds quickly. "I understand if you do."

I peer into her brilliant blue eyes, not immediately answering.

If I continue spending time with her now that I know she's leaving, it'll only be harder when we say goodbye. But I've said it since that very first hit. This woman is a drug. I'll keep coming back for more until I have no choice but to let her go.

But I *will* let her go.

"Seeing as I only have a little more time with you…" I hook an arm around her waist and tug her against me, "I'm going to need to get my fill."

I crush my lips to hers, a vice squeezing my heart

at the idea that this will be one of the last times I'll ever taste her. That I'll ever feel her. That I'll ever hear her tiny moans.

But this is how it needs to be. Any time I question if I made the right decision, all I'll have to do is look at the door to the nursery and remember what it feels like to lose my entire fucking world.

# TWENTY-NINE

## *Jude*

I stand behind the bar and look out over the packed taproom. It feels like the entire town is here. I'm not surprised. After all, it's Abbey's last night of work. If you can even call it work, considering she hasn't poured a single beer or taken a single order.

It doesn't bother me.

All these people wanted to stop by and say goodbye before she leaves in two days.

Two fucking days.

That's all the time I have left with her.

After I urged her to take the job and she told me when she'd need to leave, it seemed like a lifetime away.

But those ten days went by in the blink of an eye.

Now, in less than forty-eight hours, she'll leave Sycamore Falls.

All because I refuse to give her a reason to stay.

I keep telling myself I'm doing the right thing. I don't want to be the one to hold her back from an amazing opportunity that pays a ridiculous amount of money.

And that's the part I struggle with. She may not have come right out and said it because I wouldn't let her. But she'd give it all up for me in a heartbeat.

If I would stop being such a coward.

"You look like hell."

At the sound of Finn's voice, I pull my attention away from Abbey, my brows furrowing as I take in my brother's disheveled appearance. His dark hair is unruly, and it looks like he hasn't slept in a few days, his eyes red and droopy.

"Did you have a fire last night?" I grab a glass and place it under one of the taps, then set the honey brown ale in front of him.

He nods his thanks, then takes a sip. "I've been off. Working a twenty-four tomorrow, though."

"Then…"

"You ever feel like you're about to do something that could either be the best or dumbest thing you've ever done?"

"Every damn day," I answer with a low chuckle. "What's on your mind, Finn?"

"I'm thinking about offering to help Genevieve have a baby."

My jaw practically falls to the floor.

Of all the things Finn could have said to explain the reason he looks like shit, this is the absolute last.

"I'm going to need you to back up and tell me what you mean."

I swipe a pint glass off the counter and fill it up with a Belgian-inspired whitbier. I normally don't drink while I'm working, but I think this warrants an exception.

"She wants a baby, but after her divorce, she has absolutely no desire to date. She decided to have a baby on her own."

"So….what? You're going to provide a sample?"

"Not exactly," he says somewhat sheepishly as he tips his glass back, downing half the beer.

"But…" I shake my head in confusion. Then the realization dawns on me. "She's going for a more… natural approach."

"It's a mistake, isn't it?" He buries his head in his hands.

Despite my shock, there's something about this that's quintessentially Finn — always willing to help those he cares about. And complete strangers, too. After all, he's a firefighter.

"I didn't say that. I just…" I sigh, taking a sip of beer as I try to wrap my mind around all of this. "How did this even come about?"

"She's been looking into her options, but her insurance only covers certain things. And they require her to go through six rounds of IUI before they'll even consider covering IVF."

"What's IUI?"

"Intra-uterine insemination."

"Right."

"Her insurance has a high deductible she needs to meet before they'll cover anything. Even then, they'll only cover the procedure, not the donor vial. And each vial can cost about two grand."

Beer sprays from my lips. "Damn. Maybe I should donate sperm."

"I said the same thing. But the chances of getting pregnant with IUI are only slightly better than going the natural route, so she'd have to spend upwards of fifteen grand just to be eligible for IVF. Then there are all the shots."

"Shots?"

"Yeah. She'll have to stab her ass or thigh or something with a needle."

"All for the chance to have a baby?"

"For some people, it's the only way they *can* have a baby. But..."

"Yes?"

"She doesn't have fertility issues, so it's possible..."

"For her to conceive naturally," I finish.

"She has a fucking list."

"A list?"

"Of potential baby daddies."

"At least you made the first cut," I chuckle.

As crazy as this scenario is, I'm grateful for the distraction from my own problems for a change.

"That's the thing…" He tilts back his beer and guzzles the rest of it. "I didn't." He slams his glass onto the counter.

"What do you mean?"

"I wasn't on the list. I'm her best friend and I wasn't on the goddamn list."

I slide him a fresh beer, hoping it will help ease the tension. "Maybe she doesn't want to do anything to ruin your friendship. If she's going to be a single mom, she'll need to lean on people for support. She'll lean on *you* for support."

"And I told her I'd give her all the help she needs. Changing diapers. Midnight feedings. Whatever. But to learn she's okay with taking DNA from Mitchell Brighton? Or…or fucking Thomas Hubert? I'm sorry, but I think my DNA is infinitely better. I doubt they've got the swimmers to seal the deal."

"There's no guarantee yours are any better."

"My swimmers are just fine. I had them tested."

This additional piece of information causes me to spit out my beer yet again, leaving me momentarily speechless.

"You're really serious about this. Aren't you?" I ask softly.

He runs a hand down his face. "I don't know. One

minute, I'm convinced it's a horrible idea. The next, it doesn't seem so bad. We get along great. We practically live with each other as it is. She trusts me, and if she's going to try to get pregnant naturally, shouldn't trust be the most important factor? Or am I crazy for even thinking about this?"

"I don't think you're crazy. I think you're a good friend. Gen's lucky to have you."

I place a hand on his shoulder and squeeze, wanting him to see the meaning in my words. Then I pull back, leaning against the back of the bar.

"Look, I'm not going to tell you what to do here. If you're this worked up over it, you probably already know what you want. You're just looking for someone to give you permission. There's only one person who can do that." He narrows his gaze on me. "And I'm looking at him."

He takes another long sip from his beer, seeming to toil over my words. Then he clears his throat. "Enough of my bullshit. What's going on with yours? How are you handling things with Abbey leaving?" He brings his glass to his lips, the amber liquid sloshing against the sides. "Do you plan on finally coming clean before she leaves or are you planning on being a pussy forever?"

I give him a quizzical look. "What are you talking about?"

"You know damn well what I'm talking about. Letting Abbey leave without telling her you love her."

My throat tightens and I avert my gaze. "I don't," I stammer. "It's not—"

"It is, Jude. Whether you want to believe it or not. You love her. I see it. Hell, the entire town sees it. When are *you* going to see it?"

I part my lips, searching for the words I need to tell him he's wrong, but Finn knows me better than most. I can deny it all I want, but he knows the truth.

I do, too.

Even if I wish it weren't the case.

"It doesn't matter how I feel," I say softly, swallowing hard. "I can't give her what she needs."

"Can't?" Finn asks. "Or won't?"

"What's the difference?"

"There's a big difference. One suggests an inability. The other, a reluctance."

"She deserves to move on and be happy," I tell him, repeating the same mantra I've told myself the past several days. Then I push off the counter and make my way out from behind the bar to help clear a few tables in the hopes of avoiding this conversation.

"You do, too."

Finn's response causes me to pause in my tracks.

Can I ever truly be happy?

Can I put myself through that again when I know how it feels to have that happiness ripped away?

I scan the taproom, easily finding Abbey amongst the sea of people. I wish I could give her what she wants. What she deserves.

I just don't know if I'm ready. If I'll ever be ready.

I've spent the past several years drowning somewhere between anger and denial. I'm not sure I'll ever be able to pull myself back up above water.

Not anymore.

# THIRTY

## *Abbey*

The sun dips lower in the sky, casting a warm, golden light over everything as Jude navigates his truck up a winding road. I have no idea where he's taking me, but I don't care. All I do care about is spending time with him.

Today's been perfect, almost like a real date — ice cream from the little shop on Main Street, a trip to the farmer's market, and even a brief stop at the bowling alley, where I finally beat Jude, even if I get the feeling he let me win.

I told him he didn't need to take the day off, that I'd be fine packing or finishing up my goodbyes, but he insisted. While I'm glad to have this time together, each second that passes feels like a countdown to the inevitable.

After a few more minutes of comfortable silence, Jude turns off onto a narrow dirt path and carefully backs his truck into a secluded spot.

"Where are we?" I ask.

"You'll see." He jumps out of the truck and rushes to open my door.

I take his hand and let him guide me toward an overlook. The view leaves me speechless.

The town of Sycamore Falls spreads out below us, bathed in the glow from the setting sun. The shimmering lake mirrors the colorful sky, while the majestic mountains stand tall in the distance.

"This is incredible…," I exhale.

"Just wait until the sun goes down," Jude whispers, sending shivers down my spine. "It's even more beautiful."

"Looking forward to it," I say with a mixture of excitement and sadness. He leans in to kiss me, and emotion bubbles in my throat at the reminder that this will be my last sunset in Sycamore Falls.

"Come on." He leads me back to the truck, pulling several blankets and pillows from the back. After carefully arranging them in the bed, he helps me climb up.

"What's all of this?"

"I thought we could dine *alfresco* tonight. And there's no better view than this."

He pulls a bottle of wine from a basket and

uncorks it, pouring some Pinot Noir into a stemless glass before handing it to me.

"A picnic? Wine? This incredible view? Watch out, Jude. I might start thinking there's a romantic hiding under all that cynicism," I tease him, trying to lighten the mood.

To my surprise, he meets my gaze with a serious expression. "Maybe there is," he admits softly, and it takes everything I have not to break into tears. "Maybe…"

He looks at me for a long moment, like he's trying to figure something out, but then he shakes his head.

"It doesn't matter."

I push down the deflated feeling in my heart, and we indulge in fruit, cheese, as well as a few mini sandwiches.

I want to say something — tell him how much this means to me, how much *he* means to me — but I don't. I don't want to ruin what little time we have left. Not when he already made it perfectly clear he can't give me the answer I want.

Or maybe he *won't* give me the answer I want.

Instead, I admire our surroundings as the sun sinks lower and the sky turns into a canvas of pink and orange, pretending this isn't our last night together. Like tomorrow isn't going to come too soon, and with it, my flight to New York and the new life I'm supposed to start.

But no matter how much I act as if this is like

every other night we spent together, I know it's not. The unbearable ache in my chest is a constant reminder of that.

"Hey…" Jude cups my cheek, brushing away a stray tear, despite my best efforts not to cry.

I've been keeping them at bay all day, but now that the sun has set on my last full day, it's becoming harder and harder.

"I don't know if I can do this," I whisper, my voice cracking.

"It'll be okay," Jude replies softly, resting his forehead against mine. "You're one of the toughest people I know. If you can bounce back after all that shit with Carson, you can survive New York City."

I want to tell him I wasn't talking about New York. That I was referring to leaving Sycamore Falls. Leaving *him*.

But before I can, his lips are on mine, his mouth moving against mine in a kiss so tender I can't help but sigh. For a guy who thinks love is bullshit, he has a funny way of showing it.

Then again, I know the truth.

He believes in love.

He's just too scared to admit it.

As he swipes his tongue against mine, he pushes me onto my back, his hands roaming every inch of my frame, as if attempting to imprint it all to memory.

I do the same, eagerly tugging his shirt over his

head and running my fingers along his warm skin. Once my own clothes are tossed to the side, I pull Jude back to me, desperate to feel him. To lose myself in him. To experience everything he's willing to give me, despite knowing how much tomorrow's going to hurt.

His eyes lock on mine as he guides his erection toward me.

But unlike all the other times we've done this, he doesn't reach for a condom.

Instead, he stares at me, a silent question within.

On a hard swallow, I quickly nod.

"Are you sure?"

I pull him closer, brushing my lips against his, all our best parts lining up. "Let me feel you. Nothing between us."

"Nothing between us," he whispers as he eases inside, filling me in a way he never has before.

It feels raw and intense and absolutely perfect.

In this moment, there's nothing else. No barriers or fears holding us back. Just two lost souls who somehow found each other when we needed it the most.

The night air envelops us as our kiss deepens, the world around us fading away until there is only Jude and me. I cling to him like he might disappear if I let go. Every touch, every caress feels like a silent plea, a desperate attempt to convey all the words left unspoken between us.

I drink in every second, trying to memorize the feel of his lips, the weight of his body on mine, the scent of his skin mingling with the warm evening air. Deep down, I know that no amount of memorization will be enough to sustain me once I leave this place.

There are no hard thrusts. No punishing drives. Instead, he holds my face in his hands, moving in such a way it makes my heart physically ache.

I close my eyes, not wanting to see the affection in his own. Not when he's made it clear it won't change things.

"Please," he begs. "Open your eyes. I need to know you're with me."

"I am, Jude," I tell him, following his command. "I'm with you."

"And I'm with you." He links his fingers with mine, pinning my hands on either side of my head, our bodies moving in perfect harmony.

We've had sex more times than I can count. But it's never been like this. Never been this big. This full of emotion. This damn meaningful.

I try to prolong it, not wanting it to be over too soon, but my body has a different idea, that familiar sensation forming low in my stomach, an inferno blazing inside me.

"Wait for me," Jude rasps against my mouth, his teeth tugging on my bottom lip. "I'm almost there."

"I'll always wait for you," I exhale, wrapping my legs tighter around his waist and moving in time with him. Electricity pulses in my veins, my body being propelled higher and higher with each thrust until I can no longer fight it.

"Always," he whimpers, his body spasming in time with mine as we ride out what will be one of our final moments of bliss.

# THIRTY-ONE

## *Abbey*

The early morning sun casts a soft golden light in Jude's room as I sit on the edge of his bed, my suitcase packed and waiting by the door. A weight bears down on my chest, the thought of saying goodbye to this place excruciating. The only thing that makes it any easier is knowing I'll have a little extra time with Jude as he drives me to the airport.

I tried to insist on taking an Uber, but he wouldn't hear of it, telling me in no uncertain terms he would be driving me.

A part of me thinks it would be easier if he didn't. If we just say our goodbyes here. But another part of me will do anything to spend as much time with Jude as possible.

With a heavy heart, I stand, inhaling his scent that

still lingers in the bedroom. Then I force myself to leave. I have to.

"Let me get that for you," he says as I descend the last few steps into the foyer, reaching for my suitcase.

The sight of him makes my chest squeeze, my heart aching. His dark hair is still damp from a shower, his facial hair neatly trimmed. But his eyes seem empty as they linger on me.

"You ready?" His voice is quieter than usual.

"Ready."

Without another word, he heads to the front door and opens it. I hesitate, taking one last look around his townhouse, wondering if I'll ever have this feeling again. This sense of comfort. Of peace.

Of home.

I follow him down the front porch and toward his truck, furrowing my brow when I see his mother strolling up the driveway toward us.

"Danielle… What are you doing here?"

"Just wanted to see you off." She wraps her arms around me, squeezing me tight. "I'm going to miss having you around."

I pinch my eyes shut, swallowing down the ever-present lump in my throat. I've come and gone from more places than I can remember. But leaving Sycamore Falls is becoming the hardest thing I've ever done. Not because of the town, but because of the people.

But I'm not sure I can stay here anymore, even if I weren't taking this job.

"Just tell him," she whispers, and I meet her green eyes, blinking repeatedly.

Does everyone know how I feel about Jude?

Grabbing my hand, she gives it one last squeeze before turning her attention to Jude, something unspoken passing between them.

The drive to the airport is mostly silent, the only sounds that of the hum of the tires on the road, the low murmur of the radio, and the occasional clearing of Jude's throat. I watch the scenery blur past the window, the town I've come to love shrinking with every mile closer to the airport.

When Jude makes the turn onto the terminal road, my stomach twists and I steal a glance at him. He's focused on driving, one hand on the wheel, the other resting on the gearshift, looking as calm and composed as ever. But I know him well enough by now to recognize the tension in his jaw, the tight grip of his fingers.

I wonder if he feels it too — this pull between us, like we're leaving something unfinished.

I know we are.

I thought I was content with my decision to keep my true feelings to myself, too afraid of his inevitable rejection to tell him. But now, as he parks his truck in the airport garage and turns off the engine, Parker's words replay in my mind. How I may regret it for the rest of my life if I don't take a risk, to hell with the consequences.

She's right.

If I don't say something now, I *will* regret it.

"Jude…" I begin, my heart racing as I peer into his eyes, trying to summon the courage I need to get through this.

"Abbey, please don't," he chokes out, his words laced with desperation. "Whatever you're about to say, I am begging you not to."

"But I have to," I manage to say, his pleading expression making it nearly impossible for me to speak. "I can't leave without being completely honest. So please. Let me say what I need to. Don't I deserve that much?"

He stares at me for several long moments, his lips tight, as if he wants to tell me no. It won't matter, though. This is something I need to do for me. I can't leave any piece of me in this town.

"I'm not taking this job because it's what I want."

His eyes darken, his muscles coiled like a spring ready to snap. But he doesn't interrupt. Instead, he waits for me to continue, his gaze fixed on mine.

"I'm taking it because I don't know how to stay here… Don't know how to stay in the same place as you with how I feel about you." I wipe away the tears forming in my eyes.

"I know it's the last thing you want to hear." The words tumble out, each one heavy with the emotions

I've been holding back for too long now. "But I can't get on that plane without you knowing. Without telling you…" I draw in a deep breath, then confess, "I love you, Jude."

The silence in the car threatens to suffocate me, the weight of my confession hanging between us.

Finally, he lets out a long breath and closes his eyes, running a hand through his hair.

"I can't be the reason you stay. *Won't* be the reason you stay."

"I'm not asking you to be the reason I stay," I whisper, my voice cracking. "I'm asking if there's any part of you that doesn't want me to go. That might feel the same way about me."

"I can't do it again," he murmurs, almost too quietly for me to hear. "I can't let myself love someone and lose them again."

The pain in his voice breaks something inside of me, and I reach out, placing my hand over his and squeezing. "You won't lose me, Jude."

He shakes his head, defeated. "I can't take that risk, Abbey. I told you from the beginning. I'm not the guy who can give you what you need. That hasn't changed because of a few weeks of great sex."

"A few weeks of great sex?" I withdraw my hand, tears blurring my vision. "Is that all I am to you?"

I meet his gaze, pleading with him to tell me the truth. To tell me I changed everything for him, like he changed everything for me. To finally be honest with himself.

"That's all you are." His response wavers, his voice betraying him. But it doesn't matter. I won't fight for someone who refuses to fight for himself. Who continues to lie to himself. I deserve better than that.

I wrench open the door and hurry to grab my suitcase from the back. But before I can, he's doing it for me, placing the bag on the ground and extending the handle.

"You don't need to walk me inside," I tell him firmly. "I can manage on my own."

"Abbey, please."

"After all, it was just sex." I spit out bitterly. "Fuck buddies don't do tearful airport goodbyes, Jude."

I grab the handle and am about to storm away, but he grips my hand, preventing me from running.

"Abbey…" My name comes out strained, evidencing how much he's struggling with this.

And I know he is.

As our eyes meet one last time, I see everything he wishes he could hide from me — his regret, his pain…*his love.*

Which is why I don't yank my hand free from his.

"I'm sorry." His voice breaks.

"Yeah," I whisper, tears streaming down my face. "Me too."

Several seconds tick by as he looks between my

face and my hand, as if debating what to do. Whether he should take a risk like I just did.

With a long exhale, he shakes his head and releases me, allowing me to walk away from him.

So that's what I do, even though each step feels like a knife twisting in my gut.

I thought rebuilding my life after Carson's betrayal was the hardest thing I'd ever have to do.

I was wrong.

Walking away from Jude is ten times worse.

Because I know he loves me.

He's just too scared to admit it.

And I refuse to sacrifice my dreams for someone else.

Not anymore.

# THIRTY-TWO

## *Jude*

The door slams shut behind me, but the sound feels hollow. Empty. Just like the rest of this damn place. I drop my keys onto the counter and toe out of my shoes, neatly arranging them out of the way. Though it hardly matters. No one's here to care. No one's been here for weeks. The townhouse is dark and silent, the same as it's been since Abbey left.

Since I was too much of a coward to fight for her. To beg her to stay.

I scrub a hand over my face, trying to shake off the exhaustion that clings to me, but it's no use. Every time I step inside this place, it's like walking into a tomb.

I glance around the living area, my eyes lingering on the little reminders of her. The mug she used to drink her coffee out of. The blanket she draped over the arm of the couch. Hell, even her familiar scent lingers in every corner.

She should be here.

But she's not.

And it's my own damn fault.

I head toward the refrigerator and open it, staring blankly at its contents — a few beers and takeout containers. I'm not hungry. Not really. I'm merely going through the motions.

Eat. Work. Sleep. Repeat.

That's how I've been surviving since Abbey walked out of my life.

Hell, it's how I survived before her, too.

Shut everyone out. Stop caring. Focus on the brewery.

It's what worked after Krista and I split.

I thought it would work this time, too.

But it hasn't.

The longer Abbey's gone, the harder it's become to fill that void.

Not work.

Not my routine.

Not even pretending I don't care.

Because I *do* care. More than I thought possible.

Deciding on a liquid dinner, much like I have every night since I let Abbey slip away, I grab a beer and twist off the cap, letting it clatter to the floor as I take a long swig. The alcohol does little to ease the ache gnawing at my chest.

Without thinking, I start climbing the stairs, my feet carrying me to the one room I've avoided for years.

The nursery.

It's the last piece of a life I never got to have, the life I'd planned with Krista before everything fell apart. Before the loss. The heartbreak. The silence.

Before she walked out and never came back.

My hand hovers over the doorknob, and I hesitate, my breath catching in my throat. This is the last thing I need right now, but something pulls me forward, a force I can't explain. Maybe I'm tired of running from it. Maybe I'm just punishing myself.

I open the door, and the air inside feels stale, untouched by human presence for too long. The crib, the rocking chair, the changing table — they're all still here, just as I left them. Waiting.

But for what? A baby that never came? A future that never existed?

I take another swig of beer, my hand shaking as I look around the room. Memories flood back — nights spent painting the walls, putting together furniture, dreaming of the life we'd have. This room was once filled with so much hope. Now it's just an empty reminder of everything I lost.

A surge of anger rises inside me, hot and uncontrollable, and I release a strangled roar that reverberates around me. In my fury, I hurl my beer against the wall, the glass shattering on impact. But it's not enough to satisfy me. It's never enough.

I grab the rocking chair and slam it against the floor with all my might, causing it to splinter and crack beneath the force. The sound of wood breaking adds to the chaos in the room, but it does nothing to quiet the rage tearing through me. My heartbeat thrums in my ears as I move to the crib next, yanking at the frame until it gives way. Piece by piece, I tear it apart, like I can destroy the pain if I obliterate everything attached to it.

But even as I rip apart all the reminders of the life I once imagined, I'm not satisfied. I form my hands into fists, punching the remnants of the furniture with all the heartache, grief, and despair I possess.

I'm about to throw the elephant lamp against the wall when I hear footsteps behind me, approaching rapidly.

"*Jude! What the fuck?!*"

Before I can take out my resentment on the innocent lamp, a pair of arms wraps around me from behind, locking me in place.

"Calm down, Jude." Beckham's voice is filled with alarm and disbelief at the scene before him.

"*Get off me!*" I struggle against his hold, trying to break free. But I'm no match for my older brother's strength, as much as I like to think I can take him.

"Your hands are fucked," he retorts sternly. "If

you want to be able to keep making the beer I know you love, you need to take a deep breath and relax."

I look down at my hands for the first time, noticing the blood marring them. They should hurt, but I feel nothing other than the debilitating pain that's been present for too long now.

Closing my eyes, I do as he asks and suck in a deep breath, trying to calm the raging storm within me.

"It fucking hurts," I admit in a pained voice.

"I know."

Beckham helps guide me down to the floor, and I lean against the wall for support, physically and emotionally drained.

"Well, maybe I don't know *exactly* how much," he continues, "but I know how painful it is to be stuck in the past. Some days…," he trails off, shaking his head. "Some days, it felt like it would fucking suffocate me."

My chest heaves as I suck in a shuttering breath. I should hate that I'm having this complete breakdown in front of him. But if there's anyone I can be myself around, it's my brothers. My family.

A nagging voice in my head reminds me I was able to be myself around Abbey, too, but I quickly silence it. Thinking about Abbey is how I got here in the first place. Right now, all I want is to forget her and move on with my life.

But I have a feeling I won't be able to.

"Want to talk about it?" Beckham asks as Finn

rushes into the room, carrying the first-aid kit he always keeps in his truck, as well as a bowl of water, and three beers.

Handing the bottles to Beckham, he squats down in front of me, attempting to clean all the cuts and scratches.

"Nothing to talk about. I'm doing what I should have done a long time ago. Getting rid of all this stuff." I try to wave my hand at the destruction surrounding me, but Finn stops me so he can continue tending to my injuries.

I suppose that's the good thing about having a first responder in the family. And if it's *really* bad, there's also a doctor.

"When most people move furniture, they don't attempt to shatter it into pieces first," Finn jokes, cutting through the tension.

"I may have gotten a little carried away," I admit, taking the beer from Beckham's outstretched hand and swallowing a large gulp.

"A little?" Finn scoffs.

"This isn't about the nursery," Beckham comments quietly. "It's about Abbey."

"Don't," I grit out, taking another long sip of beer to dull the throbbing ache consuming me. And it has nothing to do with the sting from the tweezers Finn's using to dig out a few splinters.

"You let her go, Jude," Beckham continues, not

backing down despite my request he do so. "Just like you let Krista go."

"I didn't let Krista go," I snap, my voice harsh. "She left me."

"Did you give her a choice?" he counters. "After losing the baby, you checked out. Pushed her away. Pushed everyone away. All so you wouldn't have to feel that pain anymore. She left because you didn't give her a reason to stay. Just like you didn't give Abbey a reason to stay."

"I didn't want to hold her back. Didn't want to be her reason for staying."

Finn skillfully removes yet another splinter from my knuckles. "You were that reason, whether you wanted to be or not," he remarks softly. "And now you're going to let her walk out of your life because you're scared of loving her and losing her. Just like you lost Krista. And your baby."

"Aspen," I say through the lump in my throat.

"What's that?" Beckham asks.

"We were going to name her Aspen."

Silence settles in the room. In what was supposed to be Aspen's room. Instead, she never left the hospital.

If I could have traded places with her, I would have. I didn't realize that kind of love was possible until I laid my eyes on her tiny face, only to have her whisked away to the NICU, where doctors tried everything to save her, to no avail.

My brothers are right. I shut down after that. Thought if I stopped loving, I'd stop hurting.

I never did.

I lost Krista because of it.

Am I willing to lose Abbey, too?

"You think you're protecting yourself by shutting everyone out," Finn continues, "but all you're doing is building a prison for yourself."

"Let me tell you from experience," Beckham says with a self-deprecating laugh, "prison is not somewhere you want to be."

I look at the destruction around me, at the mess I've made. Not just here, but with Abbey. With everything.

"You can try to avoid love all you want," Finn says. "Can even claim you don't love her, but we know you, Jude. You adore that girl. No amount of refusal will change that."

"I tried to do that with Haley," Beckham chimes in, sipping on his beer. "Sorry to be the one to break it to you, but that shit doesn't work. Are you willing to let Abbey walk away and find someone else, all the while wondering what would have happened if you hadn't been such a goddamn pussy?" He smirks. "Sound familiar?"

I groan. "You're an asshole for throwing my own words back in my face."

"But they worked. Made me realize I wasn't

willing to let Haley go. Now I'm hoping they'll make *you* realize you're not willing to let Abbey go."

"What you and Krista went through…," Finn begins, "was fucking awful. I'm not trying to make light of it or say your grief wasn't warranted. It was. Still is. But ever since Abbey walked into your life, you've been different. I've seen the old Jude again. The Jude who joked and enjoyed the little things in life. That's what Abbey did for you, whether you want to admit it or not. She brought you back to life. Made you live again. If you ask me, that's something worth taking a risk on."

I don't answer. Just stare at the wreckage surrounding me, the weight of everything pressing down.

I wish I could tell him he's wrong, but I can't. I've been running from my pain for so long, I've forgotten how to stop. Forgotten how to live.

Maybe it's time to finally put it all behind me.

Maybe it's time to stop running and start living again.

# THIRTY-THREE

## *Abbey*

The subway rattles beneath me, the rhythmic clatter of wheels on the tracks somehow louder than usual. Or maybe I'm just exhausted.

I lean my head against the cold metal of the seat and stare at the flickering overhead lights. The train is packed with bodies pressed against each other, the air heavy with the smell of sweat. The hum of conversation buzzes in my ears, everything too loud for my taste.

I close my eyes and try to picture Sycamore Falls. The quiet streets lined with shops and smiling faces. The rustling of the wind through the trees, carrying with it a sense of peace and tranquility. The distant sound of the frogs croaking in the middle of the night, their melodic tune lulling me to sleep.

For a second, I can almost smell the clean air. Can taste the rich, frothy beer on my tongue. Can feel the soft whisper of Jude's lips against my skin.

All too soon, the subway jerks to a stop, and the sound of the doors hissing open brings me crashing back to reality. I sigh and pull myself to my feet, my legs heavy as I follow the mass of people spilling out of the car.

When I emerge onto the street, the city is alive around me, even at this late hour. The relentless frenzy of traffic and conversation surrounds me, reminding me I'm only one small piece in this massive puzzle.

I keep my head lowered, trying to block out the noise, but it's impossible. Everything's louder here. Bigger. Like the city is always moving. Always demanding attention.

I hurry past concrete building after concrete building, each one looming high above, cutting into the night sky like jagged teeth. It's all so overwhelming. This place. This life I've been trying to convince myself I want.

Yet, all I can think about is how much I miss the quiet. The open space. The stars sparkling brightly in the night sky over Sycamore Falls.

I miss the way time seemed to slow down there, like you could actually breathe. Like you had room to think.

I miss walking down the street, everyone I ran into

welcoming and friendly, even if they were complete strangers.

But more than anything I miss *him*.

I cross the street, dodging a group of tourists huddled together, staring up at the skyline in awe. There was a time I felt that way whenever I visited a big city. The excitement, the energy — it all seemed so full of possibilities with a new adventure around every corner.

Now it just feels hollow. Like I'm running on autopilot, going through the motions without really feeling anything.

Like I don't belong.

As I turn the corner onto my block, I pass a bar with people spilling out of it, laughter echoing in the air. It reminds me of Jude's taproom, though nothing here could ever feel as warm or welcoming. I quicken my pace, wanting nothing more than to escape the noise, the crowds. I just want to be alone, to shut everything out.

When I reach my building, I glance up at the windows — rectangles stacked on top of each other, all full of people living their lives in a city that's swallowed me whole.

Fumbling for my keys, I find them and unlock the door, heading for the elevator. It's a slow climb to the sixth floor when all I want to do is crawl into bed and hope for a better day tomorrow.

But when the elevator finally opens into the

hallway and I step out, I come to an abrupt stop when my gaze falls on a figure sitting outside of my apartment.

His head rests against the wall, his eyes closed. He looks worn, his usually sharp features softened by something I can't quite put my finger on. He looks so out of place here, making me think I must be dreaming.

"Jude?" I whisper, worried the dream will end and he'll disappear the second I speak.

But he doesn't.

Instead, he jumps to his feet, his deep brown eyes locking on mine. For a moment, we simply stare at each other in silence. I can't find the words, too stunned, too overwhelmed by the sight of him here, in this city, outside my door.

Then I notice the bandages on his hands, and I rush toward him, grabbing them in mine without thinking. It doesn't matter how much he hurt me. I'll always care about him.

"What happened? Was there an accident at the brewery?"

"I got into a fight with a crib." He chuckles, the raspy sound hitting me in places I wish wouldn't react to him. "I guess you could say the crib won. Or maybe I've been letting the crib win for too long now."

I release him, shaking my head. "I don't—"

"Can we go inside and talk?" Jude interrupts,

gesturing toward my apartment. "There are things you deserve to hear, and I'd rather your neighbors not have a front-row seat."

"Sure." I turn toward my door and unlock it, hyperaware of his presence mere inches away as we step inside.

Flicking on the light, I lead him into my tiny studio apartment. Since this building is mainly used for short-term rentals, it lacks any personal touch or charm — plain white walls with art prints you'd probably find at a medical office.

"Nice place," Jude remarks, breaking the silence.

"It's awful," I shoot back as I drop my bag onto the floor. "I'll find something better eventually."

I toe out of my flats and shrug off my suit jacket, draping it over one of the barstools by the kitchen peninsula.

"How did you find me?"

"Dylan."

"Of course." I laugh nervously, unsure how to act around him, all things considered.

"I wasn't sure you'd want to see me," he admits, shifting his weight from one foot to the other. "But I had to come."

"Why?"

"Because I fucked up, Abbey."

"Is this about your fight with the crib or…"

"This is about us," he says, grabbing my hands in his.

"Us?" I swallow hard, my heart hammering in my chest.

He takes a deep breath, his unwavering gaze fixed on mine. "I was a coward, Abbey. A complete idiot. I thought I was doing the right thing by letting you go. I thought if I pushed you away, I'd prove to myself I was okay without you. That I..." He licks his lips nervously. "That I don't love you."

"Jude..." I exhale, emotion tightening my throat.

"I'm scared, Abbey." He cups my cheeks, his grip firm and resolute. "I've been scared since the moment I met you. Scared of how much I care. Scared of what it means if I let myself feel this way again." His voice cracks and tears glisten in his eyes. "I lost every-thing once before. I thought... I thought if I let you in, I'd lose you too. So that day at the airport when you told me how you felt, I just... I couldn't let you in. In my mind, if I made sure you got on that plane and walked out of my life, I'd be okay."

"Are you?"

He chokes back a sob. "I've been anything but okay since I let you go. I thought I was protecting myself. I shut everyone out because I thought it would be easier. It only made things worse."

He briefly looks to the ceiling, his vulnerability shining through. Then he returns his gaze to mine.

"Krista didn't leave me," he confesses. "I left her. Maybe not physically, but emotionally. The day before she filed for divorce, I found her in the nursery, packing up everything. She said she couldn't live with that room taunting her. Instead of listening to her and giving her what she needed, I snapped. After that, I stopped living."

His voice trembles, the heartache he's done everything to bury for years spilling from him.

"And then you walked into my bar in that ridiculous wedding dress…"

I laugh through my tears, affection swelling in my chest.

"I knew nothing would ever be the same again." He curves toward me, his mouth hovering over mine. "You brought me back to life with your ridiculous optimism. And I don't want to go back anymore, Abbey. I've been living in that fear for so long, I didn't know how to live any other way." His voice drops to a whisper as he confesses, "Losing you is worse than any fear I've ever experienced. I'm done running. Done pretending. Done existing. I want this. Want us. Please tell me it's not too late."

With gentle fingers, he wipes away my tears. Then, without a single ounce of uncertainty or fear, he declares, "I love you."

My heart races as I stare back at him, unable to formulate a single response. Everything I wanted to hear, everything he's been too afraid to admit, is spilling from his lips.

"I know this is a lot for you to take in." He steps away, pacing the small space in front of me. "And I don't blame you if you have reservations, but I'm willing to do whatever it takes. I'm not asking you to walk away from this job. We'll find a way to make it work. I'll fly out here every weekend. Whatever you want."

"But you hate the city."

He stops in front of me. "I can't truly hate it. Not if you're here."

"What if I want to come to Sycamore Falls?"

"We can make that work, too. Take turns. One weekend, I'll come here. The next, you can come to me."

"And if that's not good enough?"

"I know I fucked up and I—"

I grab his hand, cutting him off. "What if I don't just want to spend a few weekends a month in Sycamore Falls? What if I want to spend every single day there?"

"But your job, Abbey. Isn't this what you wanted?"

I shrug, realizing how much my priorities have shifted. "I thought it was. But I fucking hate it," I confess. "This isn't what I want. Not anymore."

After everything blew up with Carson, I promised myself I'd never be dependent on another person again. But Jude's not just any other person.

He's *my* person.

"Then what *do* you want?" He drags my body into his.

"You, Jude," I say without hesitation. "Jobs come

and go. But you… I can probably travel all over the world and never find another man who infuriates me but makes me happy like you do."

"So what does that mean?" he asks somewhat hesitantly.

I drape an arm over his shoulder and lift myself onto my toes, brushing my lips against his. "That means I want you to take me home."

He exhales deeply, like he's been scared to breathe for too long. Then he pulls me even closer, barely a whisper between us as he murmurs, "I'm already home. *You're* my home, Abbey. And the love of my fucking life."

"I thought love was just an illusion," I tease.

"What can I say…" He tips my chin up, forcing my lips to meet his. "You made me a believer."

Then he kisses me, and for the first time in my life, I know this is where I'm meant to be.

Not in New York. Not in the corporate world.

All my life, I've wanted to feel like I had a home. A family. Like I belong.

I finally do.

# THIRTY-FOUR

## *Abbey*

The road stretches out before me, lined with familiar trees and buildings leading me through the heart of Sycamore Falls. A year ago on this very day, I sped down this same road, heartbroken and angry, trying to outrun a truth I didn't want to face. I thought I had hit rock bottom.

Funny, I didn't realize that rock bottom was exactly where I needed to be in order to rebuild.

And that's precisely what Jude and I have done since he came to New York and begged for another chance.

The first thing he did when we returned to Sycamore Falls was put his townhouse on the market. As bittersweet as it was for me, Jude needed this. If we were to have the fresh start we deserved, he needed a clean slate.

We bought a house in an adorable residential community a few miles from downtown with a stunning view of the mountains. Every evening after work, I love sitting on our back deck with Jude, watching the sunset paint the sky with vibrant colors I didn't think possible in nature.

But I don't work for Jude anymore, although sometimes we indulge in some heated boss-employee roleplay when I stop by to visit.

Shortly after I arrived back in Sycamore Falls, I received an email from one of the many nonprofits I applied to, asking if I had any grant writing experience. Luckily, I did. And the best part is I'm able to work remotely, only needing to go to their Los Angeles office on rare occasions. It's the perfect job for me right now while I settle into this new chapter of my life and figure out what I want my future to look like.

For now, I'm happy to just enjoy the moment.

As I approach the stop sign on Main Street, my foot eases off the gas and I slow to a gentle roll. The sun casts a warm glow on the familiar street with its quaint shops and picturesque sidewalks. My lips curve up at the reminder of what happened in this exact spot one year ago.

I've often wondered what my life would look like if I hadn't been pulled over and learned that Carson had reported my car as stolen. If I hadn't spotted the taproom and decided to go for a drink.

If I hadn't met Jude.

I can't imagine my life without him in it.

I used to roll my eyes whenever someone would say "everything happens for a reason." How could there be a reason for my mother abandoning me? Or my father treating me like an inconvenience?

That all changed a year ago. If one thing were different, I wouldn't be here. I wouldn't have found Jude.

I wouldn't have found my home.

After coming to a stop and checking for traffic, I step on the gas and continue through the downtown area, relishing in the feel of the wind in my hair.

Until I hear an all-too familiar beep of a siren.

My heart sinks as I glance into the rearview mirror and see Chappy's cruiser signaling for me to pull over.

Cursing my luck, I comply and move toward the curb.

"What's wrong, Chappy?" I ask as he approaches. "I didn't blow the stop sign. And this time, I own the car. Even have the registration to prove it."

"I don't doubt that."

"Then—"

"Can you step out of your car for a minute?" he asks with a mischievous look.

"Why?" I reply, but do it anyway, since Chappy's become a good friend over the past year.

"Someone wants to ask you something." He gestures toward the park where Jude found me that first night.

My pulse increases when I see him standing there, dressed in a crisp button-down shirt and slacks — a far cry from his usual attire of a t-shirt with the logo of his brewery and jeans.

"What's going on?"

"Why don't you go find out?" Chappy grins before walking back to his cruiser.

Butterflies dance in my stomach as I turn from my car and make my way toward the park. Much like last year when I got pulled over, several locals watch me with interest. At least this time, I'm not wearing a wedding dress. I still feel on edge, though. Uncertain.

"What are you doing here, Jude?" I ask somewhat nervously as I approach him. "I thought I was supposed to meet you at the taproom."

He gives me an easy smile, his eyes filled with more love than I thought possible for a man who once tried to argue that love was bullshit.

But over the past year, he's proven time and again how deep his love for me goes. He's shown it in the way he's supported me as I started my new job. He's shown it in the way he's made me an equal in our relationship from the very beginning, something I never felt with Carson. And he's shown it in the way he's made me a priority in his life, even while expanding his beer label.

"I figured we'd get a head start on our anniversary celebration."

"What did you have in mind?" I ask, the tremble in my voice betraying my nerves.

"I've actually been toying around with a few ideas." He flashes the same smile that melted my heart the first time I saw it, his dimples popping.

That smile was the first glimpse he gave me of his softer side.

Now I look forward to seeing it every day.

"Like what?"

"First, I thought maybe I'd take you to a party at Kaplan Farm, since it's pretty much a rite of passage for all Sycamore Falls residents."

"A keg party in a cow pasture," I coo. "If that doesn't scream romance, I don't know what does."

"I agree." He chuckles. "Still, I thought maybe you'd prefer something else to commemorate the anniversary of your historic getaway, so I thought we could celebrate by going to the go-cart track and having a bit of a race."

"A choice between a kegger and a go-cart race? How's a girl to choose?" I joke.

"I thought it might be tough. Which is why I settled on my third option."

"And what's that?"

"This."

He drops to one knee, causing a gasp to escape.

I knew he was up to something, considering he obviously bribed Chappy to pull me over in the exact place he did last year.

But this?

I never expected this. Didn't think he'd want to go down this road. Like I've told him time and again, I don't care if we ever take this step. I just want to be with him, as his girlfriend, wife, life partner. It doesn't matter.

Taking my hand in his, he looks up at me with those deep brown eyes I fell for the instant we met. The world fades away and it feels like it's only us.

"A year ago, a runaway bride walked into my bar. Some might say that sounds like the beginning of a really bad joke. For me, it was the start of something I hadn't expected." His words catch in his throat and he swallows hard before admitting, "It was the start of my life."

Tears well in my eyes and I struggle to choke back a sob as he pours out his heart, giving voice to his feelings. It's a stark change from last year when he kept them locked up tight.

"I've loved you since the moment you burst through those doors, even if I was too afraid to admit it at first. Since then, my love has only grown stronger with every day.

"You make me want things I never thought possible. You make me want to have a family. You make me want to grow old with someone. You make me want to have it all. So please, Abbey. Let me have it all with you. Marry me."

He retrieves a black velvet box from his pocket and flips it open to reveal a stunning round-cut solitaire that sparkles in the sunlight. I've never seen anything so beautiful. And I'm not talking about the ring.

I'm talking about the man kneeling before me.

"I thought love was a horrible reason to get married," I tease, recalling our first conversation during my bachelorette party.

His eyes shine with adoration. "You've proven me wrong before. I'm hoping you'll prove me wrong again."

"I'm pretty sure I can." I beam.

"Is that a yes?" Hope builds in his eyes.

"That's a yes," I confirm, tears of joy streaming down my face.

Without hesitation, he slides the ring onto my finger before jumping to his feet. The sound of cheers and applause fade into the background, his lips crashing against mine as he holds me like he never plans on letting me go.

As he's proven time and again, I know he won't.

Not anymore.

Thank you so much for reading *Resisting My Roommate*.

Wondering if Finn's best friend will accept his offer to be her baby daddy? Find out today in *Friends with Baby Benefits*!

**My best friend was never supposed to find my list of potential baby daddies. Now he's begging me to add one more name to the list... His.**

Just type the link into your web browser or scan the code with your mobile phone.

https://getbook.at/FriendsTL

Want one last taste of Jude and Abbey? Then sign up for my mailing list to get a digital bonus chapter. Just click the link or scan the code below.

https://geni.us/RoommateSignUpTL

Thank you so much for taking the time to read this book. If you enjoyed it, please let your friends know by leaving a review so more people can fall in love with Jude and Abbey.

# FRIENDS
## *with Baby*
# BENEFITS

***My best friend was never supposed to find my list of potential baby daddies. Now he's begging me to add one more name to my list... His.***

After my divorce, I was done with love. No more dating. No more relationships.

But I still want a baby.

IVF? Way too expensive.

That leaves one option. Finding someone with good genes, no strings, and no complications.

Simple, right?

Until my best friend and hotshot firefighter, Finn Lawrence, stumbles across my list of potential donors and suggests I add one more name…

*His.*

It makes sense. We trust each other. We have history. And there's no chance of heartbreak.

So we make a deal. No romance. No expectations. And when it's over, we go back to the way things were.

Except now, Finn looks at me like I'm something more.

His touch lingers.

His kisses don't feel awkward.

And when I fall asleep in his arms, I start to wonder if Finn Lawrence was never meant to be just my best friend.

Maybe he was meant to be my everything.

# ACKNOWLEDGMENTS

Thank you so much for reading *Resisting My Roommate*. I hope you enjoyed reading Jude and Abbey's story!

Before I sign off and start working on Finn's book, I wanted to take a minute to thank all of the people who help behind the scenes.

First of all, a big thank you to my family — Stan and Harper Leigh. Thanks for your unwavering support and also making me laugh, especially Harper when she asks if the book I'm writing has "crush business" in it.

To my wonderful PA, Melissa Crump — thanks for everything you do to keep me as organized as possible.

To my fantastic beta readers — Melissa, Stacy, and Vicky — thanks for always reading for me and offering feedback, even on such short notice. I'd be lost without you ladies.

To my admin team — Melissa and Vicky. Thanks for keeping my reader group and page running.

To my review team — Thanks for reading and reviewing my books. Your support means the world to me.

To my reader group — Thanks for being my super-fans and giving me a place to go when I need a break from writing.

And last but not least, a big thank you to YOU! Thank you so much for picking up this book and taking a chance on it. Whether you've been a long-time T.K. Leigh reader or are just finding me now in this new genre, I'm so happy you took the time to read my words.

Next up is Finn's book, and I CAN'T WAIT!

Love & Peace,
~ Tracy

# ABOUT *the* AUTHOR

Tracy Leigh is the spicy small town alter ego of USA Today Bestselling author T.K. Leigh. She lives outside of Raleigh with her husband, daughter, special needs rescue dog, and three cats.

When she's not penning her next small town romance filled with heat and heart, she can be found reading, spending time with her family, or planning her next escape to Hawaii.

facebook.com/tracyleighbooks

instagram.com/tkleigh

tiktok.com/@tracyleighauthor

bookbub.com/authors/t-k-leigh

pinterest.com/tkleighauthor